She smiled and, opening her mouth, she touched her tongue to his lips seeking more. His lips parted and she tasted him.

Everything about him felt right. Heat flooded her and she gave in to his demand, sighing in surrender as she wrapped her arms around him and sank into a depth of passion she'd never known before. Wanting more, she pulled him closer.

He slanted his head, taking the kiss deeper, the fever higher. He threaded his fingers through her hair, holding her still for him while his thumb feathered softly over her temple in a soothing caress.

She nipped at his lower lip with her teeth. She wanted that hand, both his hands, lower, tracing her curves, igniting a true fire between them. She pressed closer trying to show him, and a squeak sounded between them.

"Oh, my goodness." In an instant everything came flooding back.

The crash.

The toddler.

The man.

No, no, no. She'd let a man touch her. Almost as bad, she'd been smooching with the prince!

Dear Reader,

World building is one of the exciting aspects of being an author. In this book you will revisit Pasadonia, the principality I created for *The Making of a Princess,* and then move to a new kingdom of Kardana in the North Sea. I felt it was better to create my own countries than mess about in others when dealing with royal families.

Some of my favorite scenes in this book are when the characters travel by train. I hope you enjoy your luxury ride. Those scenes were particularly fun for me to write because I have a friend who occasionally caters on a privately owned train car. I've listened to her stories of trips through the years and finally put it to work for me. Jill, thanks for the inspiration.

Happy reading,

Teresa

Stolen Kiss
From a Prince

Teresa Carpenter

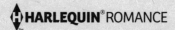
HARLEQUIN® ROMANCE

Recycling programs
for this product may
not exist in your area.

ISBN-13: 978-0-373-74286-8

STOLEN KISS FROM A PRINCE

First North American Publication 2014

Copyright © 2014 by Teresa Carpenter

Printed in U.S.A.

Teresa Carpenter believes in the power of unconditional love, and that there's no better place to find it than between the pages of a romance novel. Reading is a passion for Teresa—a passion that led to a calling. She began writing more than twenty years ago, and marks the sale of her first book as one of her happiest memories. Teresa gives back to her craft by volunteering her time to Romance Writers of America on a local and national level.

A fifth-generation Californian, she lives in San Diego, within miles of her extensive family, and knows that with their help she can accomplish anything. She takes particular joy and pride in her nieces and nephews, who are all bright, fit, shining stars of the future. If she's not at a family event you'll usually find her at home—reading, writing or playing with her adopted Chihuahua, Jefe.

Recent books by Teresa Carpenter

THE MAKING OF A PRINCESS
BABY UNDER THE CHRISTMAS TREE
THE SHERIFF'S DOORSTEP BABY
THE PLAYBOY'S GIFT
SHERIFF NEEDS A NANNY
THE BOSS'S SURPRISE SON

This and other titles by Teresa Carpenter are available in ebook format from www.Harlequin.com.

This book is dedicated to the new generation in my family, which will include a new baby boy and a new baby girl when this book is published. Alliyah, Faith, Sabina, Amare, Walter, and Ryann, you are my inspiration. I love you all and wish you all the best.

Teresa Carpenter believes in the power of unconditional love, and that there's no better place to find it than between the pages of a romance novel. Reading is a passion for Teresa—a passion that led to a calling. She began writing more than twenty years ago, and marks the sale of her first book as one of her happiest memories. Teresa gives back to her craft by volunteering her time to Romance Writers of America on a local and national level.

A fifth-generation Californian, she lives in San Diego, within miles of her extensive family, and knows that with their help she can accomplish anything. She takes particular joy and pride in her nieces and nephews, who are all bright, fit, shining stars of the future. If she's not at a family event you'll usually find her at home—reading, writing or playing with her adopted Chihuahua, Jefe.

Recent books by Teresa Carpenter

THE MAKING OF A PRINCESS
BABY UNDER THE CHRISTMAS TREE
THE SHERIFF'S DOORSTEP BABY
THE PLAYBOY'S GIFT
SHERIFF NEEDS A NANNY
THE BOSS'S SURPRISE SON

This and other titles by Teresa Carpenter are available in ebook format from www.Harlequin.com.

This book is dedicated to the new generation in my family, which will include a new baby boy and a new baby girl when this book is published. Alliyah, Faith, Sabina, Amare, Walter, and Ryann, you are my inspiration. I love you all and wish you all the best.

CHAPTER ONE

PRINCE DONAL'S PLANE GOES DOWN IN WORST STORM OF THE CENTURY

Today the world prays as superstorm Allie rages, hindering search and rescue attempts from reaching the plane carrying Donal and Helene Ettenburl, Prince and Princess of Kardana. The royal couple left the principality of Pasadonia traveling with other dignitaries for a weekend of skiing in the French Alps. There was no indication when the plane left Pasadonia that the two cold fronts pouring rain and snow over most of Europe would collide into an ice storm. The death toll is in the hundreds and continues to grow as utility outages leave hundreds of thousands without power. A distress call came from the royal flight late Saturday morning and there has been no contact since. French officials have elite search and rescue teams ready to go as soon as weather conditions allow. Prince Julian Ettenburl met with the French officials and rescue teams en route to Pasadonia to be with his nephew, the royal couple's thirty-two-month-old son, Samson Alexander Ettenburl, who remained behind, a guest of the Pasadonia royal nursery. On the plane with Donal and Helene Ettenburl were...

JULIAN FLIPPED THE news screen off with a sharp flick of his thumb and dropped his phone in his pants pocket. He knew his purpose for being in Pasadonia. Knew the plans for rescue included not only France's best cold weather rescue crews, but Kardana's as well. He'd provided the best vehicles, the best equipment, the best people available to find his brother and the future king of Kardana.

The news of the crash nearly killed his father, already frail from a mild stroke a year ago. Julian needed to gather his family and return home as soon as possible. And that included his brother, lost on the side of a mountain. For now he'd settle for his young nephew.

The train trip, the only mode of transportation capable of managing any distance in the storm, had been interminable but had allowed him to make the arrangements for the searchers. Though Prince Jean Claude had invited Julian to wait out the storm in the comfort of the palace, Julian preferred to begin the return trip. He hoped the nursery staff had Samson ready to go.

He arrived at the nursery and was greeted with subdued courtesy by the Matron, a pleasant woman, her plump figure and serene smile giving her a motherly appearance.

"Your Highness. May I express my wish that your brother and all those on his plane will be found soon, safe and sound?"

"Thank you. May I see my nephew?"

"Of course. But Master Samson is sleeping." Matron advised him. "I hate to disturb him as he's been restless and distressed missing his parents. You may see him, but I recommend letting him sleep."

"Thank you, Matron." Julian inclined his head in acknowledgment of her comments. Fading sunlight flooded the large room through the many windows. Colorful rugs covered the gold marble floor, while masterpieces of fanciful art graced the walls. White furnishings added a crisp cleanliness to the room. He spotted three attendants besides the matron. He had no doubt Samson had received the best of care in these rooms.

"It is my desire to return to Kardana as soon as possible. Please have the Prince's things packed and ready to go. And have his nursemaid report to me." He was surprised not to spy Tessa, Samson's nursemaid, somewhere nearby.

She always seemed to be hovering about, eyeing him. With the encouragement of his sister-in-law. Tessa was a dear friend of Helene's, and always struck Julian as more of a companion than a child care specialist. He made it a point to avoid them both.

Now he hoped for Helene's safety.

"It's best he return home," he advised the woman before him.

Matron nodded. "It is good he will have people around him he knows. However, he is quite exhausted and likely to be very fussy if you wake him now. Might you wait for a bit?" Her gaze cut to something behind him and back again as she made her plea. "Perhaps after you have dined?"

"Unfortunately, time is an indulgence I cannot allow. Please take me to my nephew," he demanded, denying her request for a delay.

"Of course." With a sigh, she gestured toward a door behind him that led to another room.

In here the drapes were closed and the lights turned low. Samson slept in a low race-car-shaped bed in the west corner. An older child occupied a canopied daybed nearby. As Julian stood over him, Samson jerked in his sleep and his tiny brow pinched as if stress followed him into slumber.

So young.

So innocent.

So important.

Looking down on him, Julian felt totally inadequate to care for him. The thought that he might be responsible for raising this child to be King outright terrified him. He was a bachelor by choice. He liked his tranquil life behind the scenes. Being Minister of the Treasury suited him, the numbers, the strategy, the quiet.

One more reason to pray for his brother's safe return.

"Julian, *ami*." Princess Bernadette, a regal blonde, swept into the room. She flowed forward and embraced him in warm arms, kissing the air over both cheeks. "I am so sorry. Tell me you have good news of Donal and Helene?" He shook his head, his gaze going to the thin woman with short platinum blond hair, who followed the Princess into the room. Tessa. Good.

"There is nothing new to report. The weather prevents a full-scale search. America sent a SEAL team to help. They are leading a small group of extreme weather experts on an extraction expedition, but it is slow going and communication is spotty."

"At least it is something." She squeezed his hands. "Please know we pray for their safe return."

He nodded an acknowledgment. "You can understand I am anxious to return to France to oversee the rescue operations."

"Indeed." She looked down on Samson. "Poor baby knows something is wrong. He has been fussy. He will be happy to see you. He needs the familiar and to be with family."

Right. Julian couldn't remember the last time he'd held the child.

"Thank you for your care of Samson. It has been a relief during these trying hours to know he is in good hands. Now, however, we have a train to catch." He nodded to the bed. "Tessa."

With a flick of pale blue eyes, the nanny stepped up to the crib and reached for the toddler. Samson jerked awake. Blinked at Tessa then Julian and let out a scream.

A shrill scream woke Katrina Vicente. She sprang up in the small bed, her fuzzy mind immediately going to Sammy. The toddler wasn't dealing well with his parents' disappearance. He totally rejected his nanny. The dolt, and Katrina didn't use the word lightly, had told the boy his parents weren't coming back. Of course he went into hysterics.

Tessa quickly realized her mistake and had tried to correct herself by telling him his parents were lost and everyone was looking for them, but the not-yet three-year-old didn't comprehend the nuances of the situation. All he knew was he wanted his mama and papa, and they weren't here.

From that point on he wanted nothing to do with Tessa. She was familiar but not his mother, and he was smart enough to know when he saw her it meant his mother wasn't back yet.

Hearing his screams she pushed to her feet, ready to take on the dark-haired man who'd dared to wake her charge.

"*Mon Dieu*." She rushed forward. "You best have a good reason for waking this child. Or I'll have your head." She sent a chastising glare toward the Matron, hovering behind the man's broad figure.

"K'tina." Sammy twisted toward her voice and held out his arms.

She reached for him, the pitiful wail wringing her heart.

"Who are you?" The man stepped back, turning so Sammy was beyond her grasp. He stared down his aristocratic nose at her. The deep timbre of his voice easily cut through Sammy's renewed screams even as the boy thrashed wildly in his arms. "Samson, be still, child."

"I am the one who got him to sleep." She'd worked so hard to get him settled. In total despair, he hadn't been sleeping or eating. The poor baby was completely out of sorts.

He'd been in the middle of a screaming fit when Katrina came on duty early the day before. As nursemaid to the children of Prince Jean Claude and Princess Bernadette, she had become well adept at soothing such scenes. She'd wrapped him in her arms and sang softly to him. He shrieked and thrashed, but she'd held him securely, rocking and singing as he cried. Finally he'd slept for a couple of hours. Bringing much-needed peace to the nursery.

From then on he'd latched onto Katrina and she'd gladly stayed to care for him. She managed to calm him some, got him to eat a little through the day, but he rarely slept more than a few minutes at a time before he woke screaming. Nightmares, Dr. Lambert diagnosed.

And now this man had awoken him from his first decent rest.

"He's going home," the man stated.

"Give him to me." Undeterred by the man's imposing stance, she invaded his space to reach the boy. Focused on the child's cries, she tried to take Sammy, but quickly learned she was no match for the man's strength.

"It's okay, baby." She stroked Sammy's light blond hair seeking to reassure him. "It's okay. Katrina is here."

"Mama!" Sammy cried out at the same time he threw himself backward in the man's arms.

Unprepared for the sudden movement, Katrina was unable to elude him, and his hard head conked into hers. Pain exploded across her temple and black dots grew into bigger dots until darkness threatened to overcome her. She swayed and felt a hard band circle her waist. Slowly the dimness receded, and she found Sammy was in her arms and she was in the stranger's. Her legs felt weak yet she had no fear of falling. In the background voices buzzed.

"Katrina!"

"My goodness."

"Call the doctor."

Sammy clung to her, his small head resting on her chest, his wails growing into full-fledged screams. Disoriented, she blinked up into rich amber eyes.

"I have you." Warm breath tickled her neck. He led her to the daybed she'd been sleeping in until a few minutes ago. "Sit. We must check out your head."

"Sammy first," she insisted, grateful to be off her feet. Though curiously disappointed to lose the security of his arms. The bump on the head obviously distorted her thinking.

Dr. Lambert arrived within minutes. Light bounced off his bald head, and bushy white eyebrows topped expressive eyes. He smiled kindly and spoke in English, the official language of

Kardana. "How is our little man tonight? I hear he actually got some sleep before trying to knock you out with his head. I'll want to look at you, too."

"I am okay, but Sammy has a sizable knot on the back of his head." She sent Prince Julian a chastising glare. Oh yeah, she'd finally recognized the gorgeous, dark-haired man. "But, *oui*, he slept for a couple of hours before he was disturbed."

"Well, let us see what the damage is."

The doctor had been by to see Sammy every day, so he didn't try to move the toddler from her lap. Instead he talked gently to the boy, telling him what he was doing and why. He felt the child's head, looked into his eyes and listened to his heart. And when he was done with the boy, he did the same with Katrina. Again without disrupting Sammy.

"Did you lose consciousness?" He shone a light in her left eye.

"No." Katrina carefully kept her attention on the doctor and not the tall, brooding man standing arms crossed over a broad chest on the periphery of her vision.

"She came close," a deep voice put in.

The reminder brought to mind the feel of his strong arms cradling her. She'd been pressed against his hard body, the warmth of his masculine heat reviving in her moment of weakness. The memory sent blood pounding through her veins, adding to the throb in her head.

She didn't care for the thought of spending the night in the medical wing, so hopefully the doctor wouldn't attribute her racing heart to the bump on the head.

No, that came from the brilliant action of telling the Prince of Kardana she'd have his head for waking his nephew.

Not that she hadn't meant the reprimand at the time. Sammy needed the rest. But he also needed family. Ever since Tessa disclosed his parents were missing, Katrina had taken to following the doctor's example of talking to Sammy, explaining what had happened and what was being done to find his parents. It seemed to calm him.

He may have a limited vocabulary, but he understood a lot more than he said.

The one thing she'd promised him, again and again, was his family would come for him and then things would be better. He'd be with people who loved him, who would care for him, who would do everything they could to bring his parents back to him.

Unfortunately Julian Ettenburl didn't quite fit that picture. *Warm and loving* were not words she'd use to describe him. *Cold and stoic* fit him better. And impatient. Though that was more a feeling than anything he did.

His utter stillness revealed nothing of what he felt, nor did his fine-hewed features or his intelligent hazel eyes under straight brown eyebrows. His brother was touted as the handsome one, being blond and eye-catching. A soldier in the royal corps, he was seen as a man of action, a man in control. The world viewed him as a true Prince Charming.

Julian was darker, his features more defined, his demeanor more brooding, a testament to his preference to shun the limelight. Having seen them both, Katrina found the younger brother more attractive if infinitely less charming. She ducked her head, not that she had any interest in him, or in any man.

She had little doubt the dark prince would wield his considerable power and influence to find his brother. Sammy, however, might get lost in the shuffle as his uncle concentrated on the bigger goal.

"A bit of a concussion for both of you." The doctor sat back and regarded her and Sammy. "And you're both exhausted. I recommend twenty-four hours rest at the minimum."

"Can he travel, Doctor?" Julian asked, squaring his shoulders into an even-sharper line. "He can rest on the train."

Katrina tensed at the suggestion. Sammy stirred against her, and she patted him softly, adjusting so she covered his ear with one hand while lightly running her fingers through his hair with the other. Surely the man didn't intend taking Sammy tonight?

"Your Highness, I understand your urgency to return to France and the search for your brother, but the boy is traumatized. He was told his parents weren't coming back."

At this news amber eyes met hers, his disapproval drilling deep into her. No question who he blamed. She swallowed hard but refused to look away.

The doctor went on. "Sammy is in distress. The staff has done their best, especially Katrina, but he's slept and eaten little since news of the crash reached us. With the addition of this head injury, I highly doubt he'll get the proper rest he needs on the train."

"Julian—" Bernadette moved to the prince's side "—we have rooms ready for you. Why not stay the night and see how Sammy is in the morning? The early train is at eight, not too big a delay."

No mention was made that if the inclement weather continued, travel might be impeded. There was no need. It didn't take a genius to figure the odds, and it was well-known that Julian

Ettenburl was off-the-charts smart. Yet after only a few minutes in his presence Katrina saw he wasn't a people person.

Why ever had he been the one to come for Sammy?

She supposed it spoke well of him. But not if he insisted on making the child travel before he was ready. A glance from the Princess had Katrina biting back her opinion.

He showed some sense when he nodded at Bernadette. "We shall stay the night. Though I would like Samson with me."

"Of course." Bernadette readily agreed as she sent Katrina a hopeful glance. "Your suite has two rooms. I'll have a crib set up in the second bedroom."

"Thank you. You are most gracious."

"I do hope you'll join us for dinner. Jean Claude has been closely monitoring the rescue operations. I know he would welcome a chance to speak with you."

"As I would him." The Prince sighed, showing the first sign of weariness. "Actually, I find I'm quite famished."

"Then we shall dine." She hooked her arm through his and drew him toward the door. "Our chef will be pleased with the opportunity to impress you. Unless you'd prefer to freshen up first?"

"No, that is fine." He paused to nod at Tessa. "Please see Samson settled into my rooms." His critical gaze slid over Katrina. "I prefer you resume his care."

"Of course, Your Highness." Tessa bowed her head in acquiescence.

Heat flooded Katrina's cheeks at his obvious censure. Arrogant beast. She was happy to see the back of him as Princess Bernadette led Prince Julian from the room.

Tears stung the back of her eyes. Exhaustion, she knew. She didn't usually let attitude get to her. She lived in a world of royalty, worked in the palace, where arrogance and entitlement were practically job requirements. She'd learned long ago not to let it bother her.

Tonight, as she fought to keep her eyes open, it hurt.

Dr. Lambert righted her when she listed to the side. "My dear, you need to find your bed."

"*Oui.*" Oh how she craved her own bed. But first she'd see to Sammy, despite his uncle's wishes. She wouldn't let his poor behavior dictate hers.

"Good, you're going to be sensible. Just as well you live here in the palace. With the concussion, you'll need someone to check on you periodically through the night."

She'd like nothing more than to follow the doctor's orders and head to her room, but in the past few days Sammy had stolen a part of her heart. He'd brought her back to life. She couldn't rest until she knew he was settled for the night.

"What about Sammy?" Tessa asked. "Should I wake him during the night?"

"Yes. Wake him and check his pupils. If you notice any oddities or if he starts vomiting, call for me."

Tessa nodded and reached for the sleeping Sammy. He awoke with a jerk and shrank away from his nanny with a weak cry.

Katrina stood, cradling him to her chest. He subsided against her, closing his eyes. "I will carry Sammy to the Prince's rooms and see him settled."

Tessa blocked her way. The nanny looked down her nose at Katrina. "I'll take him."

She eyed the taller, thinner woman. It hadn't skipped Katrina's notice the other woman had kept her silence when the Prince focused his blame on Katrina for Tessa's lapse of judgment in telling Sammy of his parents' disappearance. In Katrina's opinion, the woman was showing no better sense now than she had before.

"I do not think so." She moved to walk around the woman.

Again Tessa stepped into her path. "His Highness made it clear he wishes me to resume my duties. He will expect me to deliver Sammy to his rooms."

Sighing Katrina shifted Sammy in her arms, his deadweight beginning to weigh on her. "Look, I am too tired to deal with a crying fit because you want to impress the Prince. He is not even in his rooms. Let me put Sammy down. We all know he is more likely to go back to sleep if I do it."

"Sammy is my responsibility." Tessa continued to protest.

"And in a minute I am going to give him to you and go to bed." In no mood to argue, Katrina pushed past the woman. Sometimes exhaustion had its advantages. "Think about it. Would you prefer Prince Julian come back to a sleeping child or one awake and wailing in misery?"

Tessa had no response for Katrina's challenge because they both knew she spoke the truth. Which didn't mean Tessa accepted it graciously. As they fell into step behind the porter showing them to Prince Julian's rooms, every click of her heels shouted her dissent.

Let her sulk. It was Sammy Katrina cared about. Her head throbbed and her arms began to burn, but one look down at his innocent, tearstained face gave her the strength to continue on. In the end they arrived at the suite before the crib did, and she gratefully sank into a blue silk tufted chair.

The room, a lavish display of antique elegance in blue and gold, reminded Katrina of what she loved about the palace. Tradition and longevity were built right into the brick and mortar of the royal home. She remembered coming here with her father as a child and thinking the palace was the most beautiful place on earth. She'd had so much fun with the other kids in the nursery she'd told papa she wanted to come back and live here someday.

Three years ago, she moved in. She never dreamed it would be under such agonizing circumstances.

But she worked hard, and last year earned a position in the nursery. She loved working with the children. Especially the royal twins, Devin and Marco. Because of her black belt in karate she was often assigned to them. The three-year-old boys were full of mischief and mayhem, yet were so smart and loving they were impossible to resist.

Katrina jolted from a light doze to find Tessa standing over her. She blinked and saw through the open bedroom door off to the right that the crib had been set up.

Good. The last thing she needed was another encounter with the headstrong Prince.

CHAPTER TWO

JULIAN ABSENTLY SHREDDED a piece of bread, unable to focus on the fine meal provided by the palace's talented chef.

He kept reliving the moment when his nephew shrank away from him with a cry of distress. It tore at his heart both as the child's probable guardian and as a man. He and his father were the child's closest relatives. Samson should be reaching for him not seeking comfort in the arms of a stranger.

Even if those arms were soft and scented of apple blossoms. Or if the stranger protected him fiercely with flashing violet eyes and a fiery mane of bouncing curls. The woman barely reached Julian's shoulder, and she'd been ready to personally take his head for disturbing Samson's sleep.

Probably a guilty conscience.

Fury fried already-frayed nerves at the thought of the meddlesome chit causing Samson undue trauma by telling him his parents wouldn't be returning. Even if it proved true, that should have been his job and handled once the boy was back among family. And after Julian had a chance to discuss the matter with a professional so he knew the best way to approach the issue without doing the kind of damage Samson was currently experiencing.

"My friend, you should eat," Jean Claude, Prince of Pasadonia, urged him. "The next few days will be trying. You will need to be at full strength."

"The meal is delicious." Julian speared a succulent shrimp from the savory dish. "I apologize for my lack of appetite." He usually valued a gourmet meal, but preoccupation prevented him from fully enjoying the multicourse fare. Nonetheless he appreciated the royal couple's efforts. Plus they'd provided a safe haven for Samson during the travesty of the past two days.

Physically anyway. They obviously needed better trained nursemaids.

A soft touch settled over his fingers, and he looked into Bernadette's sympathetic gaze. "I know you have much on your mind. I cannot imagine how you are holding together."

"It is difficult," he agreed, wondering if he should pull his hand away from hers or just leave it until she retreated. He respected the offer of solace, but her touch made him uncomfortable.

These awkward moments were why he preferred to avoid social situations.

"I hope you know we support you whatever the outcome of the search." Jean Claude spoke bluntly. "Of course we hope the rescue will be successful, Donal and Helene are in our prayers, but I know you are already preparing for the worst. If there is anything I can do to help, you have only to ask."

"You know me too well, my friend."

He'd met the older man when he was fourteen and Julian's family visited Pasadonia to witness the crowning of the new ruler, Prince Jean Claude Antoine Carrere. He'd been kind to an awkward kid on an occasion when he could be forgiven for being overwhelmed by his own agenda. Their relationship had grown through the years, and Julian looked on Jean Claude as one of his closest friends and advisors. The fact he was a well-respected world leader only added to the value of his offer.

"My mind boggles at all that must be done. But in truth I cannot focus on anything beyond finding Donal."

"Understandable." Jean Claude nodded. "I have my experts watching the weather and will provide you with any updates as soon as I receive them."

"I appreciate it." Julian chafed again at the

delay keeping him from returning to France. "I'm anxious to get back to the rescue operations."

"Yes. It is unfortunate that Sammy's condition has delayed you. It is admirable of you to put his needs first. He has had a difficult time missing his parents."

Julian clenched his jaw in irritation. "It was upsetting to learn he'd been told of the crash."

"It was not intentional," Bernadette rushed to assure him. "Tessa—"

"Excuse me, Your Highness." Jean Claude's assistant appeared at his side and handed him a folder. "The current weather report. And the call you were waiting for is holding."

"I shall be right there." The Prince glanced at the report and then handed it to Julian. "Not much change. I have to take this call. We will talk before you leave in the morning. Bernadette."

The Princess gracefully stood and rounded the table. She stopped and kissed Julian's cheek. "Stay. Finish your meal. A porter will show you to your room."

He cleared his throat. "Don't worry about me."

She sighed. "But I do. Good night, *mon ami*. If you wish to get some air, use the courtyard. The press are everywhere."

The Prince and Princess left the room hand in hand, an obvious unit set to deal with whatever business awaited them.

For a moment Julian envied his friend. Usually an insular man, it might be nice to have someone to talk to right now. Due to his father's frail health, Julian couldn't burden him with his worries, and it would be inappropriate to discuss family affairs with outsiders.

No longer hungry, he followed the porter to his room. When the elevator opened on his floor, Samson's cries pinpointed Julian's destination.

He rushed forward then waited impatiently for the porter to open the door. Inside he found Tessa walking Samson, both were in tears. Julian briskly made his way toward the two only to come to a dead stop next to them. What to do?

"What's the problem?" he demanded.

"The doctor advised me to wake him and check his pupils. Only he wouldn't go back to sleep. He started crying, and nothing I've done has helped."

"K-k'tina." Samson's breath hitched on the wail, but his message was clear.

"He keeps asking for her," Tessa revealed, the plea in her eyes as heart wrenching as Samson's tears.

Julian set his back teeth. The woman had caused this problem; it went against everything in him to reach out to her for help.

Feeling helpless, watching both woman and child struggle, he racked his mind for something to do to right the situation. But for all his considerable knowledge and his massive IQ, he lacked experience dealing with women and children, let alone both in a state of distress.

Considering distraction to be an option, he tried to take the boy.

"No!" Samson screamed and hit out at him. "K'tina!"

Bloody hell, he rebelled against drawing that woman back into his nephew's life. She was the reason he suffered so. But this wasn't just a tantrum; this was a miserable child seeking solace from the one person he'd connected with during this crisis. How did Julian deny him?

Simple, he didn't.

He called for a porter seeking information about Katrina and found that she had rooms at the palace. Lucky for him or he'd be out scouring the streets of Pasadonia. He soon stood outside Katrina's room. He wished for a more formal form of address, but in all the confusion they hadn't been properly introduced.

A maid answered his knock. She bowed. "Your Highness."

"I need to see Katrina." He stepped past the maid into the room.

"She's sleeping," the young woman said softly. "I've followed the doctor's orders. I woke her just half an hour ago and she was fine."

"I'm not here about her injury."

Through the open door of the bedroom he saw the redhead. Light from the lounge fell across the bed and the lovely woman within it. Long lashes dusted creamy pale cheeks. Dark bruises under her eyes were a violation against the porcelain perfection of her features. Whatever she'd done, he couldn't deny she'd pushed herself beyond the expected to help Samson.

Suddenly it seemed wrong to ask more of her. But for Samson he must.

"I'm sorry to disturb her, but I need Katrina to come with me. My nephew needs her help."

"Oh." The woman looked uncertain and then nodded. "I will wake her." She slipped inside the room and closed the door.

He paced the small lounge, wishing he were anywhere but here.

People called him cold. And maybe he was. If preferring order and calm were attributes of being cold. He needed both to do the work he did. Overseeing his country's treasury, including both finances and security, required a clear head and a focus of purpose.

He could work under pressure but he rarely had to. He had the ability to see the big picture, to track patterns and trends. So he prepared and diversified and created contingency plans. Which allowed him to move before the market did.

Some said it was magic or worse called him

psychic. Bah. It was just the way his mind worked. He enjoyed learning things, and his brain absorbed knowledge like a sponge. He surprised himself with the facts he knew sometimes.

People, on the other hand, were a mystery to him. As was their penchant for displaying high emotions.

A bachelor at thirty, he'd been content in his role as the spare heir. Though his father occasionally addressed his desire for Julian to find a suitable woman and start a family, the pressure had lessened after Donal wed Helene and Samson was born.

Still, Julian was a man like any other, with the same needs. His position, however, called for discretion. He managed that by having a number of lady friends he escorted to the many functions his title forced him to attend. By spreading his attention around, no one—women or press—built up undue expectations.

He supposed his reputation for being cold kept him from being dubbed a playboy.

The woman, Katrina, threatened his hard-won detachment. His attraction to her stunning beauty just made him angrier over the whole situation. As did the intelligence he'd spied in her violet eyes. She struck him as being too smart to make the blunder she had. So what had she been thinking?

Shock, he imagined. But it was no excuse, not in her position.

He may not be able to do anything to help his brother, but he could make sure Samson was cared for. And if that meant disturbing the injured woman's sleep, he'd do it without remorse. She deserved no more rest than the child she'd traumatized.

The door opened and Katrina walked barefoot into the lounge. She wore a lush white bathrobe that brushed her bare pink-tipped toes. Under it was a white garment trimmed in lace cut nearly as low as the V of the robe.

His gaze jerked to hers from the soft swell of her breasts visible in that V. She was so pale there was very little difference between her skin and the white of her nightclothes. Except for the shadows he'd noted earlier.

"Is Sammy okay?" she asked in a voice husky from sleep, her brow furrowed in concern. "Have you called the doctor?"

"His injury is not the problem," he assured her, his brusqueness more for his benefit than hers. "Tessa woke him as instructed, but he will not go back to sleep."

She gave a resigned nod, the action making her head appear too heavy for her slender neck. There'd been no sign of softness or frailness when she attacked him in the nursery. Just fierce protection of Samson.

Now he saw how tiny she was, clearly no more than five-four at the most. At six-two he towered over her. The oversize robe didn't help. Nor did her fiery mane of hair, which she'd tamed into a braid that hung halfway down her back. But without makeup, her skin appeared starkly white against the vibrant color of her hair.

"Shall we go?" She moved forward, swaying slightly.

He ground his teeth, half tempted to send her back to bed. More than tempted to join her there. He dismissed the inappropriate thought, disgusted with his libido for rising up when his full attention should be on his brother's family.

Samson's needs came first.

"Where are your shoes?" he demanded, focusing on the practical.

She stopped and frowned, as if it took an effort to think. He was reminded she, too, had taken a knock to the head.

"I'll fetch them." The maid disappeared into the bedroom and returned a moment later with a pair of fuzzy slippers. Katrina slipped them on; her pink-tipped toes peeked through the end.

She rubbed her forehead. "Would you prefer I take the time to dress?"

Yes. There was something entirely too intimate about her in nightgown and robe.

"No." Again he thought of Samson, saw tear trails on pale cheeks. "Let's go."

He followed her from the room and was surprised when the maid also stepped into the hall.

"It is all right, Anna." Katrina bid the maid. "Thanks for watching over me. You can go now."

"Oh, but I have doctor's orders," the young woman protested.

Annoyed by the delay, Julian bit back his impatience to address the woman. "What are your instructions? I'll see she's cared for the rest of the night."

Clearly upset with the change in circumstances but unable to countermand his authority, Anna outlined the doctor's instructions. "You must wake her every few hours and ask her questions to make sure she is coherent. If she's not, or you notice anything strange about her pupils, or she gets sick, you need to call the doctor immediately."

As she spoke, he automatically looked into Katrina's eyes to check her pupils and found himself lost in the solemn depths. Blinking, he turned to the maid, acknowledged her instructions and sent her on her way. While he took care of that, Katrina started ahead of him.

Her actions caused him to scowl. Protocol demanded she follow him. Sighing, he decided to cut her some slack; she had a concussion after all. However, it didn't escape his notice she appeared to know the way.

Though it may only mean she'd asked after where Samson would be, Julian believed it was more than that. She'd probably been the one to put him to bed. He wasn't okay with that. He'd charged Tessa with taking the boy to his rooms, made it clear he'd wanted her to resume care of the boy.

Already his authority was being undermined. Something he would not tolerate.

"Mademoiselle—" Damn. What was her name? He quickly closed the distance between them. "I wish to make myself clear. Your assistance with Samson is appreciated. That does not mean I will abide interference with my decisions regarding his care."

"Of course," she responded as she pressed the button to call the elevator.

"Are you mocking me?" he challenged, crowding her.

She blinked those big violet eyes at him as she shrank back, making him feel as if he'd chastised an innocent.

"No," she said, and entered the elevator. She moved into the corner, her toes curling into her slippers. She pulled the edges of her robe together and tightened the sash. "I know you want what is best for him." A wan smile lifted the corner of her mouth. "Otherwise I would not be here right now."

He searched her features for any hint of guile but saw only the ashen evidence of her exhaustion. She looked so fragile he thought of sending her back to her bed. Only the thought of Samson's suffering kept him resolute.

"Excellent." The elevator doors opened and he waved her forward. "As long as you understand."

They traveled the remainder of the distance in silence. Which made the sound of Samson's cries all the more grating as they approached the door to Julian's rooms.

Inside the suite, tears stained the cheeks of both Tessa and Samson. The nanny had been walking the boy, trying to soothe him, but upon his and Katrina's arrival, she began sobbing.

"I can't take anymore." She thrust Samson into Katrina's arms and fled.

Katrina didn't hesitate. She wrapped Samson close and started talking to him. "Hey, baby, it is fine. I am here. Does your head hurt?" She kissed his light curls. "Mine, too."

Though he continued to cry, there was no denying Samson preferred the redhead to the blonde. Instead of fighting the embrace by curling up and putting his arms and legs between his body and Tessa's, he clung to Katrina's lusher figure.

Finding the scene painful to watch, knowing this might just be the beginning of Samson's trials, Julian moved to the fireplace to start a fire. This was going to be a long night.

Katrina continued to coo to Sammy until his sobs lessened and eventually he sat up in her arms. She used the collar of the fluffy robe to wipe his pale cheeks. Poor baby, he had such a hard road ahead of him. Ever the optimist, even she had to acknowledge the chances of his parents surviving both the crash and the icy weather were long odds.

Still, she prayed and she hoped. Miracles happened every day.

"Mama? Papa?" Samson asked around a shaky breath.

Biting the inside of her lip, she shook her head. "We do not know yet."

Tears leaked from his eyes. "I want Mama."

"I know, baby. She wants to be with you, too. And look…" She walked to the fireplace where Prince Julian stood. "Uncle Julian has come to get you." She met brooding brown eyes. His discontent with her conversation showed in the stiff set of his shoulders. He'd soon learn Sammy did better with information than platitudes. "He is going to take you to where they are looking for Mama and Papa, and then he will take you home."

"Unca Julie." Boy studied man for a minute then surprised her by holding out his arms indicating he wanted to go to his uncle.

Julian's eyes went wide when she plunked the toddler in his arms.

"Uh, hum." He cleared his throat, clearly at a loss what to do with the boy.

"It is a good thing." She mouthed the words, not wanting to disturb the moment. Though she stayed close enough to be enveloped in the dual scents of manly musk and baby shampoo.

This was the first time Sammy had voluntarily gone from her to someone else. It showed a level of trust that boded well for the future.

"Mama? Papa?" He put the question to his uncle.

Julian paled. She understood his pain. It broke her heart every time she had to tell Sammy his parents weren't coming home yet.

Julian's gaze shot to her.

She shrugged and crossed her arms over her chest. "Talk to him. He is a sharp biscuit. He does not talk much, but he understands more than you might think."

Skepticism flashed over his aristocratic features before he turned his attention to Sammy.

He hoisted the child up in his arms so they were eye to eye.

"Samson," he began, and for a moment she worried he'd lecture the young Prince on duty and decorum. But Sammy's intent attention must have swayed him. "The best searchers in the world are looking for them." And then he added. "I want to see them, too."

More tears leaked down Sammy's cheeks. He reached out, grabbed Julian's ears and leaned his forehead against his uncle's. The two shared a moment of loss and hope.

The poignant picture had Katrina swiping at her own cheeks.

Emotion must have gotten to Julian, because he squeezed too hard causing Sammy to squirm. He turned and held his arms out to her.

She looked to Julian, hating to end the closeness between the two, but he seemed happy to hand Sammy off to her. Hoping the exchange was enough to allow the boy to settle into sleep, she carried him into the room where the crib had been set up.

He frantically shook his head and began to cry. "No. No tired."

Rather than force it she backed up. Right into a hard male body.

"Oh!" She swung around even as his hands went to her waist, and suddenly she found herself in the Prince's arms. She looked up, and up, past his stubborn chin to eyes of molten gold. Oh yeah, definitely the better-looking brother. And way too close.

"Sorry." She winced internally at the squeak in her voice as she stepped back. Or tried to. His fingers tightened on her waist, holding her still as his hot gaze strolled from the gaping neckline of the robe to the racing pulse in her neck, to the bite she had on her lip, to her eyes. She played it cool even as a shiver traced down her spine and her pulse raced.

Wrong time.

Wrong place.

Wrong man.

Wrong woman.

He obviously agreed, because his hands dropped and he stepped aside.

Breathing a sigh of relief she moved past him to pace the room. Julian moved to the fireplace to stoke the fire. Way wrong man. She'd spent enough time in the palace from childhood on to know the demands placed on royalty. And the price was too high. If she ever worked out her trust issues, she wanted a kind man and a simple life.

Two strikes against Prince Julian.

Okay, that wasn't totally fair. These weren't

the best circumstances. Obviously he was under a lot of pressure.

Her arms were beginning to burn from fatigue so she took a seat on the antique sofa and tucked Sammy comfortably against her. He denied it, but he was tired. Part of his objection was probably to the crib. He hated to be called a baby. But what he really craved was human contact.

Calling to mind one of his favorite stories, she began a tale about a train named Thomas while slowly running her fingers through his baby-fine blond hair. After all he'd been through, she hoped it wouldn't be long before he fell asleep.

Thanks to Julian. He might be brusque and rude, but she gave him points for putting Sammy's needs before his own. She knew he would have preferred to leave Pasadonia without ever seeing her again. Or more on point, without Sammy seeing her. Yet he'd come for her rather than let Sammy cry himself into exhausted slumber.

She smothered a yawn, forced her eyes open and skipped ahead in the story.

So maybe there was a little kindness buried somewhere inside the cold Prince.

CHAPTER THREE

JULIAN TAPPED HIS lip as he contemplated the two asleep on the sofa. Snuggled up in Katrina's arms, Samson appeared more at peace than Julian had seen him since arriving at the palace.

Thank God. He'd taken about all of the boy's distress that he could handle.

Blast Tessa for deserting them. He was counting on her to help him with the boy on the trip home. She'd best have herself pulled together by morning. If he needed proof he was ill prepared to handle his nephew, he received it tonight. Samson couldn't get away from him fast enough.

Julian wanted to strangle Katrina when she started talking about Donal and Helene to the boy. Yet when faced with a direct question from Samson, Julian couldn't lie. Giving the child false hope served no purpose beyond delayed pain. Best he prepare for the worst and be surprised by a miracle.

Which didn't change the fact he'd be better off if left in the dark about the crash in the first place.

Julian switched his gaze to the woman responsible for some of Samson's suffering. Her lap provided a comfortable resting place for the child, but Katrina sat in the middle slumped to the right with her head listing at an angle sure to cause a crick by morning.

Dare he risk moving them? For certain they'd be more comfortable in a bed. But as he considered the logistics, he doubted the success of getting them both to the desired destination still asleep, an imperative in his mind.

He admired the Victorian design of the sofa they occupied, but nobody could argue the merits of its long-term comfort. The bench had cushioning, but the tufted back curved higher on one end than the other. Her position in the middle offered her little support on either side.

He supposed he had the answer to his earlier observation. If he were the cold bastard everyone thought him, he'd simply leave the woman and child to their own devices. When she became uncomfortable enough, she'd wake and move to the bed taking Samson with her or putting him in his crib. Problem solved.

But Julian wasn't that cold. With a sigh he rose and approached the sofa. Settling into the corner he turned toward the sleeping pair and pulled woman and child into his arms.

"Hmm." She surprised him by opening drowsy

violet eyes and staring up at him. "I am going to go to bed," she assured him in a sleep husky voice.

He waited, but instead of moving away, she snuggled into him with a contented mew, shifting her hold on Samson to keep him secure.

"You smell good," she murmured.

Him? She was the one who smelled good enough to eat, making him wish he'd eaten more of his meal. Maybe then he'd be less tempted by her.

He closed his eyes and tried to pretend he was at home in bed. He pulled to mind a problem he'd been wrestling with before the fateful plane went down and changed his life. Neither solution worked. The subtle, sweet scent of apple blossoms and the soft feel of womanly curves cuddled in his arms brought his body to life.

He ignored the inappropriate reaction.

She was exhausted and injured, and he'd accepted the responsibility of her care. That was the extent of their connection.

"You're so warm."

He shook his head, a half smile lifting the corner of his mouth. "Go to sleep already," he said running his hand over the silk of her hair.

And closing his eyes, he followed his own advice.

Deep in the night, something disturbed Katrina. She stirred slightly and then purred softly. It had been a long time since she woke up in Rodrigo's arms. How she'd missed this connection, the feel of hard arms holding her close, the warmth of a man's nearness, the sensual tickle of his breath on her cheek.

She opened her eyes to find the room dark except for the dying embers in the fireplace. Sighing, she snuggled in, hugging him as she drifted toward sleep.

He smelled so good, of musk and man. Her brow furrowed as her foggy mind niggled at a sense of wrongness, but it hurt to think. He shifted beneath her and the thought fled. She realized his movement was what woke her.

Yes. The only thing better than sleeping in his arms was being awake and in his arms. A pain in her head followed the thought. Thankfully it didn't linger and she dismissed it. Better to focus on the man. Without opening her eyes she angled her head and kissed him.

He went completely still, his sleep-relaxed body going tense. Usually he took it from there. Not tonight.

Tease. She smiled and, opening her mouth, she touched her tongue to his lips, seeking more. His lips parted and she tasted him. She knew immediately this wasn't Rodrigo.

And while her mind struggled with why that was a good thing, the man gave in to her invitation, sinking into the embrace with an aggressive dance of tongues.

No, this was not Rodrigo. Everything about him felt right. Heat flooded her and she gave in to his demand, sighing in surrender as she wrapped her arms around him and sank into a depth of passion she'd never known before. Wanting more, she pulled him closer.

He slanted his head taking the kiss deeper, the fever higher. He threaded fingers through her hair, holding her still for him while his thumb feathered softly over her temple in a soothing caress.

She nipped at his lower lip with her teeth. She wanted that hand, his hands, lower, tracing her curves, igniting a true fire between them. She pressed closer trying to show him, and a squeak sounded between them.

"Oh my goodness." In an instant everything came flooding back.

The crash.

The toddler.

The man.

No, no, no. She'd let a man touch her. Almost as bad, she'd been smooching with the Prince!

"*Mon Dieu*, I am sorry." She pushed back and checked on Sammy, who'd been crushed between the two of them.

A scowl drew his tiny eyebrows together and

his mouth twitched a couple of times, but he didn't waken. Somewhere during the night, he'd switched his weight to Julian. Without looking at the Prince, she lifted Sammy carefully and carried him into his crib. Before leaving the room she switched on the light and checked his pupils, sighed in relief when she found them even and reactive.

Unable to delay further, she returned to the sitting room, where Julian stood by the mantel stoking the fire back to life.

"Your Highness," she began.

"Stop." He put down the poker and turned to face her, keeping his hands clasped behind him. "You have already apologized. Now it is my turn."

"No, please." How mortifying. "I kissed you. It is my fault. I woke up in your arms—which it was very sweet of you to let Sammy sleep." His dark brows lowered so she rushed on. "I thought you were my old boyfriend. Oh God. You smelled wrong, but you felt good—"

"You are babbling, *mademoiselle*—" His sigh reeked of exasperation. "What is your full name?"

"Katrina Lynn Carrere Vicente." She cringed as soon as the words left her mouth.

"Carrere?" Of course the name caught his attention. "You're a relative of Jean Claude?" His tone turned grim. "Please tell me you are not related to the Prince."

"Distantly," she confessed, "through my mother." She didn't mention her father was a close personal friend. No need to make matters worse than they were.

His head dropped forward causing thick strands of hair to fall over his wide brow. He muttered what sounded like, "It just keeps getting better and better."

Her sentiments exactly.

But the show of emotion lasted only a moment. He quickly drew himself up and straightened his shoulders.

"Mademoiselle Vicente you have my deepest apologies. I should never have touched you."

"Your Highness."

He shook his head. "I'll express my regrets to the Prince in the morning."

"No." Her eyes went wide in shock. She felt sick to her stomach. The last thing she wanted was for the royal family to know she'd forced herself on a guest. She couldn't handle another disgrace. She stepped forward in entreaty. "Promise me you will not."

"I must." His posture was rigid. "I have offended a member of his family."

"No offense. None." She assured him. "You were the perfect gentleman."

His eyes narrowed in censure. "I had my tongue down your throat. Hardly the actions of a gentleman."

"But you kept your hands above my waist. I wanted them on me—" She broke off as his eyes darkened and narrowed even more. What was she saying? So not the place to go.

"I promise I am not offended. It has been a tough couple of days for everyone, and we found a moment of comfort in each other. That is all that happened."

"Is that how you see it?" His shoulders relaxed slightly.

It was all she would allow herself to believe.

"Yes. You held Sammy and I while we slept, something we both needed desperately. Something I believe you needed, too. The kiss came from the comfort of that gesture. You are leaving in the morning. Can we not forget it ever happened?"

He studied her in silence so long her nerves grew rattled. Finally he beckoned. "Come here."

Leery, she forced apprehension aside to approach him slowly, until she had to tip her head back to look up at him. He stared down into her eyes, his gaze penetrating. Again he rattled her with his intensity. Would he agree to put her indiscretion aside?

"Yes?" she prodded.

"Just checking your pupils," he stated. "How do you feel? Any nausea?"

The question confused her until she remembered her concussion.

"No," she assured him. Did he think her injury affected her thinking? No, only her actions. It was the only excuse she could come up with for her uncharacteristic advances. "I am fine."

"So it would appear." He nodded formally. "Tessa is next door. You may use the bed in Samson's room."

"Thank you." At the mention of bed, fatigue washed over her. "I checked on Sammy when I put him down. He was doing fine."

"Good. That's good." He turned back to the fire, clearly dismissing her.

But she couldn't leave without knowing if he meant to speak to the Prince in the morning. The loss of her career was the least of her worries. She respected and honored the people in this household and wished no harm or embarrassment on them. Not again.

She couldn't bear her father hearing of this. The disgrace might well jeopardize his friendship with the Prince.

"Please, Your Highness." She dared to disturb him. "I must know if you plan to reveal my indiscretion to the Prince."

He stiffened but did not turn. "It shall be as

you requested. We simply shared a moment of comfort."

"Thank you." She backed away, eager to put this encounter behind her. There was much more to Prince Julian than his reputation gave him credit for. Tonight she could only be thankful for his mercy.

Sleep eluded Julian. He worried about Donal, his father, Samson, while thoughts of duty warred with his natural inclination to stay in the background. Every instinct he possessed rebelled against losing his brother.

At five in the morning, he gave up all pretense of trying to sleep and rang for coffee, a hot breakfast and an array of items for Samson and the nanny. In anticipation of an early departure he also asked for Tessa to be roused so she could pack and get Samson ready for travel. Next he called and advised his security detail of his plans.

One of the advantages of being in the palace was not having security underfoot every moment.

He'd dressed and packed his own bag when the knock came at the door. He glanced at the closed door of the temporary nursery as he crossed the room. There'd been no movement from that quarter, a hopeful sign Samson was getting the rest he needed.

Another knock sounded as he reached the door.

He opened it to find his meal and the lady of the palace awaiting him.

"Bernadette." He bent over her hand. "You look fresh and lovely, considering the early hour. To what do I owe this honor?"

She moved gracefully into the room. "I have something to discuss with you. I am hoping I might share a cup of coffee with you while you eat."

"Of course." He waved her toward the elegant cart the steward had situated near the window and pulled the desk chair around for her use. The steward produced another chair and Julian joined her.

"Thank you, Pierre." Bernadette smiled a dismissal.

"What do you wish to discuss?" Julian picked up his napkin.

"*Non, mon ami*, you must eat first," she insisted. "You barely touched dinner last night."

"I had a lot on my mind."

"As you will until Donal is returned to us. First rule of being a ruler—take care of yourself." She lifted a dome, revealing a hot plate of steaming eggs. "Take a few minutes and enjoy a peaceful meal. Then we shall talk."

Lifting the coffeepot he poured two cups and placed one in front of her. "What you have to discuss must be really bad." He tapped his cup against hers. "I believe it's best if I eat first." He dug into his vegetable omelet.

"Wise choice." She sipped, closing her eyes and taking a deep breath of the freshly brewed beverage. She flashed him a sheepish smile. "Jean Claude prefers tea. I like both so I usually defer to him. But I do enjoy a good cup of coffee."

"There's nothing better to jump-start the day," he agreed.

She chatted while he ate, managing to avoid any sensitive topic in the process. The weather, politics and his family were never mentioned. He admired her talent at putting him at ease, allowing him a few minutes peace while he enjoyed his meal.

When he finally set down his fork, she topped off their coffee and got to the point.

"I am afraid I have some upsetting news. Tessa came to see me last night and asked me to let you know she cannot return with you to Kardana."

"What?" He carefully set his cup in its saucer. This couldn't be happening. "That is unacceptable."

"I know the timing is bad." She placed her hand over his. "However, she is very distraught. You know Helene is a close friend."

"Samson needs her."

"Unfortunately she feels too overwhelmed to

resume his care. She was in tears as she requested an escort to take her home to England."

"She's left the palace?" Shock blocked all thought.

"Yes." Bernadette confirmed, and with a gentle squeeze she released him. "I hope you will not blame Tessa too much. The last couple of days have been very emotional. Sammy rejected her after she told him of the crash. She tried to help but—"

"Wait." Julian cut her off. "Are you saying Tessa told Samson his parents were not coming back? I thought Mademoiselle Vicente made the mistake of telling him."

"Oh no." Bernadette shook her head, visibly surprised by his assumption. "We were at our wit's end with Samson when Katrina came on duty. He was inconsolable for hours. She took one look at him, gathered him in her arms and began rocking him. And she talked to him."

"About Donal and Helene." Yes, he'd seen a sample of her frankness with the child last night. "He responded to what she told him."

"He did." Her admiration for Katrina came through in her earnestness. "He stopped crying to listen to her. And he finally slept for a short time. She did not leave his side until you arrived."

Her revelation stunned him, sent his mind reeling. Something he experienced rarely. It was unlike him to make assumptions. Then again, the circumstances of the past few days were far from the norm.

The tragedy of the crash had his emotions rising to the surface, yet he was helpless to do anything. Anger at Katrina for the distress she'd caused Samson had given him something to focus on and do something about.

Erroneously, as it turned out.

Not only was his indictment and coldness misplaced, they were an affront to Katrina and the royal house that opened its arms to a hysterical child suddenly thrust upon them. He'd personally witnessed Katrina's dedication yet discounted it in favor of his preconceived notions.

He cringed inside when he realized he owed her yet another apology.

"…I truly believe it is the best solution," Bernadette said. Her expression was expectant and Julian realized she'd carried on with the conversation while he'd been examining his conscience.

"I apologize, Bernadette, my mind wandered for a moment. Do you mind repeating your solution? I am most anxious to hear your suggestion. I cannot leave Samson here, but I am far from a nursemaid. Frankly, the thought of changing a nappy is terrifying."

"Quite a vivid picture." Her melodic laughter

lightened the mood. "But I think you are safe. Sammy is potty trained."

Finally, something in his favor.

"Plus, no apology is necessary."

How he wished that were true.

"As I mentioned before, Samson has become attached to Katrina. My suggestion is she accompany you back to Kardana and stay until Tessa is ready to resume her duties or you find a replacement."

"Oh no." Horrified at the idea, he summoned a polite smile. "I could not steal off with a member of the royal family. Katrina told me of her mother's relationship to the Prince."

"Really?" Bernadette's fine brown eyebrows lifted in astonishment. "How interesting. Katrina rarely reveals her connection to Jean Claude." She tapped a finger on the table as she eyed him thoughtfully. "You must have asked her."

"I did. Why does she keep it to herself? Is it a secret?"

"Heavens no." Diamonds flashed as the Princess waved a careless hand. "Jean Claude is very fond of his goddaughter. Katrina, dear child, does not care to take advantage of the relationship."

"Goddaughter." Just shoot him and put him out of his misery. Katrina conveniently left that little tidbit out when she garnered his promise to forget his slip in protocol last night.

"Yes. Jean Claude went to school with Dom Vicente. They are the best of friends. Katrina has been tripping around the palace since she was tiny."

"Vicente." Of course he recognized the name. He should have caught it last night, but the royal name distracted him. "We've met several times. I'm surprised I haven't heard of the relationship."

"That is at Katrina's request." Concern darkened her features. "She prefers not to draw the attention of the press."

A confession trembled on the tip of his tongue. Only the fact he'd given his word kept him from disclosing his actions.

Well, that and the fact the moment seemed too intimate to share. The few hours holding her were the only solid sleep he'd had in two days. Waking to her mouth on his, her taste and scent surrounding him, drew him into the passionate interlude. Yet her reference to comfort resonated with him.

He'd agreed to forget the incident because she'd been correct. Comfort had led to the embrace. He wouldn't regret the rest, so how could he condemn them for the kisses?

"She is wonderful with the children," Bernadette continued. "We would have been happy to have her without a degree in child development, but she insisted on meeting all the qualifications and more. We often have her assigned to the twins. Of course it does not hurt that she is family and has a black belt in karate."

The more she extolled Katrina's virtues, the more the muscles tightened across Julian's shoulders.

"You have made my case, dear Lady. I cannot take away such an important member of your household."

"Julian—" her eyes shadowed with sadness "—we insist. We want to help. This is one small thing we can do. How is your father?"

He released a deep sigh. Giving his father news of the crash might be the hardest thing Julian had ever done. It was a well-kept secret the King had suffered a stroke a year ago. Mild as the stroke was, it had been a slow road to recovery, with both Donal and Julian taking on more and more of the royal duties as their father tired easily.

His father shrank before his eyes when he learned Donal and Helene were missing and presumed dead. His first thought had been of Samson. He had urged Julian to journey immediately to Pasadonia and return his heir to Kardana.

"I will not lie." Though he must be ever cognizant of keeping up appearances, "It was a blow. As you can imagine, he is anxious to see Samson."

"Yes, of course. How is Samson? I have not

heard of any complications from his bump on the head."

He imagined not much happened in the palace she didn't know about.

"Both he and Mademoiselle Vicente were fine when I checked on them around three. Grumpy but fine."

Another tinkle of laughter sounded. "For certain it is no fun to be awoken in the middle of the night. Poor Julian. You have had it tough these last few days. What news do you have from France?"

"I'm told the storm is beginning to abate, but less so at the altitude of the projected crash site. The elite team should reach the area soon. They're hoping to have more to report later this morning."

"Knowing you wished to leave early, I checked, and the train will be delayed an hour or two while they clear a couple of sections of track. I also checked the travel advisory and many roads and passes are still closed, so the train is still your best choice."

"That's disappointing." The delay chafed at raw nerves.

"Jean Claude ordered our private train car made ready for the trip. You will be more comfortable. Plus, it will save you from having to deal with the press on the trip. I know it is not what you wanted to hear, but at least the delays will give Katrina time to pack."

"Pack?" a sleepy voice asked. Julian turned toward the sound to spy Katrina coming toward them. His body stirred at the sight of her mussed red hair and sleep-tousled beauty. "Where am I going?"

"Do you really think this is a good idea?" Katrina nervously twisted the ring on her right hand as she questioned her Princess's sanity. They were in the bedroom of her suite. Katrina sat on her bed, fighting for composure as she marshaled arguments against Bernadette's calm insistence. "The press is all over this story. It is the perfect time for someone to come forward and cause irreparable damage, not only to the house of Carrere but to the Kardanians, as well."

"It is the perfect opportunity for you to learn you have nothing to fear. We worry about you, Katrina. You cannot hide in the palace forever, my dear." Bernadette folded a lemon-yellow sweater and placed it in the open suitcase. "Young Samson needs your help. It is obvious he has bonded with you. Of course we remain hopeful, but it is likely the poor child will need a strong advocate in the following days."

"It is not worth the risk. His family—"

"His family needs you." Bernadette came to

the bed and took Katrina's hands in her own. "King Lowell is rumored to be in ill health and the queen mother is in her eighties. If Prince Donal has perished in the crash, Julian will be engulfed with running the country. I fear they may lose sight of Sammy in their grief."

"The staff—" Katrina quickly changed the words at the disappointment in Bernadette's eyes "—are no substitute for family."

"No. And it may fall to you to remind them all of that. Though losing a child, a grandchild is terrible, they still have Sammy, and he is reason to persevere. Dear, I know your concern is not just for yourself."

"I would never do anything to hurt Jean Claude." Katrina rushed to assure her friend and mentor, the slip of the night before haunting her.

"I know." Bernadette squeezed her fingers. "He knows. We believe in you. It is time for you to believe in yourself. Now—" Bernadette rose and went back to the wardrobe "—let us finish packing. Julian is not a patient man."

No, patience did not describe the visiting Prince. Which only made the challenge ahead of Katrina harder. But she dared not argue further. Even she recognized there was a limit to testing a royal's goodwill.

Even her? Especially her!

She'd never been good at decorum. She'd had

too much freedom running wild about the palace as a child. Jean Claude adored his goddaughter, so she was given undo leeway. She learned her lesson three years ago when the misuse of that freedom and a lack of good judgment resulted in hurting those she loved most.

Licking her wounds, she'd retreated to the place she felt safest in the world. The palace. More specifically the palace nursery, where she tried to be a good example of decorum to the next generation.

Her stomach twisted at the possibility of bringing shame to her home once again. No matter what Bernadette said, Katrina knew she'd been a disappointment to Jean Claude, worse to her own father. She stiffened her spine. *Not this time,* she promised them in her heart. She would go with Prince Julian to help Sammy, and she'd mind her manners, follow protocol and be a model of perfect decorum.

If she stuck to the background, there was no reason anyone should notice her.

CHAPTER FOUR

KATRINA GLARED AT the broad shoulders of Prince Julian as she hitched Sammy to a more comfortable position on her hip. The man hadn't spoken two words to her since bidding the Prince and Princess farewell. Julian seemed happy enough to accept the offer of Katrina's services yet disinclined to look her in the eyes.

To the side and behind the royal party strode armed security officers of both Kardana and Pasadonia. She silently and obediently followed the directions given to her as they boarded the royal train car provided by Jean Claude. Inside, an officer stood guard over them while the rest of the Kardanian security force did a quick scan of the whole car.

She stood quietly, but Julian was obviously antsy.

"Down," Sammy demanded and wiggled in a bid to get his way.

"Not yet." She tightened her arms around him,

but he was strong and she nearly lost her grip on him.

"I'll take him." Julian cautiously lifted the boy into his arms. He met her gaze briefly. "Thank you for your patience and cooperation with the security. I know it can be trying."

"I am used to it." She shrugged. "I sometimes travel around town with the twins." Over the past year she'd ventured out twice.

"It is a pain," he declared, his opinion punctuated by the tense line of his shoulders.

"A necessary evil for your safety. For Sammy's safety," she calmly pointed out. Her closeness to the royal couple and their twins made her happy for the protection that kept them safe. "And because I am with you, for mine."

"Samson," he corrected her. "Unfortunately many people do not grasp that notion. Ha." He gave a harsh laugh, a rueful shake of his head. "This is a change. Usually it is I explaining the need for caution."

She eyed him, reluctant to be sympathetic when she was annoyed with him for ignoring her. But he had taken Sammy, who still chattered and wiggled in a bid for freedom. And generally she wasn't one to hold a grudge.

"I suppose that can be trying, as well."

"I'll tell you, it can be a real damper on a date." Long-felt aggravation rang through the words.

Her turn to laugh. "Poor baby."

He froze and looked down his nose at her. "You are impertinent, *mademoiselle*."

She flushed and looked away. "I am sorry."

"Your Highness," Neil, Julian's head of security, turned to them, "the space is secure."

"Thank you." The lift of a dark eyebrow let her know she'd been saved by the announcement. "What is your security plan?"

"A man at both entrances." The trim, dark-haired man responded. "St. James will be in the computer room, and I'll be roving. The trip to Lyon is expected to take four hours."

Julian nodded. "And the weather?"

"There's been no change. Reports indicate the storm is lessening, but the airport at Lyon is still closed."

"Keep me apprised if anything changes."

"Very good, sir." Neil bowed briefly and moved down the corridor.

Julian turned back to Katrina. "*Mademoiselle,* would you care to give us a tour?"

"My pleasure," she lied. Just a tiny fib actually. What she'd really like was to take Sammy into one of the guest rooms and sleep. Instead she followed in Neil's wake down the narrow corridor running along the left side of the train from the back where they boarded.

"The car has three guest rooms." She opened

the first door on the right and showed him a small room with a double bed, the decor a sparse elegance equal to a high-end hotel. The second door revealed a room much like the first, in reverse order with twin beds.

"These two rooms share a bath with a full shower. With your permission, I'll sleep with Sammy in here." He nodded. Good. She had the nursery monitor with her, but she preferred to stay close to the child. Unfortunately, it also put her closer to Julian. *Not a problem,* she vowed. It wasn't as if there was the least likelihood he'd make a move on her.

His appalled reaction to her kiss this morning proved she was safe from him.

"The master suite is the next door down. You have a private attached bath. The entire train car is bulletproof, including all the windows, plus the master bedroom acts as a panic room should the car be breached. I am sure Neil will go over all the specifics with you."

She waved him ahead, and he stepped into an elegant oasis decorated in cream, tan and bronze. This room included a small seating area and a bar with a mini refrigerator. Next came the lounge with plenty of comfortable seating in dark leather followed by a half bath and the crew's quarters.

Upstairs, she showed him the domed observation lounge with big-screen TV, the formal dining room, kitchen, tiny computer room and crew's lounge. As with the guest rooms and lounge below, the furnishings here were tasteful and soothing. Plush silver-gray carpet cushioned every step, soft hunter green velvet covered the couch and chairs, while dark woods, fine crystal and a stunning black marble table added to the richness of the rooms.

"Quite the setup." Julian let Sammy down in the observation lounge and settled into an armchair. "Much more comfortable than the deluxe sleeper car I traveled in to Pasadonia."

"Indeed," Katrina agreed. "Princess Bernadette especially prefers traveling by train when they have the twins with them. There are gates attached to the top and bottom of the staircases."

Sammy ran to the large curved sofa fitted into the rear point of the train. He clamored up, plopped right in the middle and gave them a wide grin.

She caught her breath and exchanged a hopeful glance with Julian. The smile was the first she'd seen Sammy give.

"You like it, too, little one." Responding to his joy, she sat next to him, lightly threaded her fingers through his hair. "Or is it the freedom you like? You have been very good today."

The train began to move, slowly pulling away from the palace yard. At the motion Sammy's eyes grew large, and he looked up at Katrina for reassurance.

"It is okay." She smiled. "This is a train. It is like a house on wheels. We are moving—turn around and you can see."

The boy climbed to his knees then stood and looked out the back. She lifted up a hand to protect him from a fall. He pointed at the palace staff seeing the train off. Several waved. Sammy waved back. "Bye-bye."

"That is correct…we are going bye-bye. We have started our journey." She thought of adding their final destination of home, but didn't want to remind him of his parents when he was in such a good mood.

Suddenly Julian settled onto the green velvet on the other side of Sammy and turned to face her. After he had ignored her for most of the morning, his scrutiny unnerved her. Protocol prevented her from questioning him. Instead she kept her focus on Sammy, playing point and name until the boy got bored of the game and slid off the couch to run around the open space of the lounge.

"I understand I owe you another apology," Julian stated gruffly.

"Oh?" Katrina wondered for what.

Several items sprang to mind, rudeness certainly, and rushing her—he'd given her a whole hour to pack and say her goodbyes. This, after Princess Bernadette practically forced him to take Katrina with him. That had been an awkward scene. She had been no happier about the idea than he was, but Bernadette wouldn't be dissuaded and Katrina felt obligated to support her Princess.

"Yes. Bernadette explained it was Tessa who told Sam—" He stopped and eyed Sammy before continuing. "That Tessa was responsible for Samson's distress. I blamed you when I shouldn't have. You have my apology."

Her brows popped into her bangs before she quickly got her disbelief under control. "Um, well. She was in a state of distress herself," Katrina explained. "I believe she and Helene were— are friends."

"There is no excuse for her behavior." There was no give in his response. "She is the nanny of a royal Prince. His welfare needs to come before any other consideration."

"I agree. The child's needs should always come first. Sammy, stop. Stay in this end of the room." She scooted to the edge of the couch, ready to hop up if Sammy went any farther. "But shock can make us do stupid stuff."

He surprised her by sweeping a thumb over her cheek. "Very generous of you, considering you have taken the brunt of her thoughtlessness."

His touch threw her more than his stare. Obviously he meant to denote the shadows under her eyes. She'd be mortified if she could think beyond the sensation of his caress. She blinked up at him, striving to recall the topic of conversation. Oh yes, his apology.

"Sammy is the one who has suffered. Though we do not truly know how much he understands. He is not yet three. He probably does not fully comprehend what *missing* means."

"He's a bright boy. I've never heard reports of him acting up in this manner." Julian turned his attention to Sammy, who was climbing into a club chair and pounding on the table. "He knows something is wrong."

"Yes," Katrina agreed, relieved and yet curiously disappointed to lose Julian's regard. "I think he is reacting to the tension in those around him. He has been different since you arrived. This is the first time he has played, the first time he has smiled. You are familiar, someone from home. He feels more secure."

"He knew Tessa."

"She was fairly new as his nanny, was she not?" At least that's what Katrina had heard.

He nodded, his features etched in grim lines. "She assumed the role a couple of months ago. A farce if you ask me. The woman has no child care training."

"But he is a Prince!" she blurted, shocked by the revelation. Tessa might be Helene's friend, but Sammy was the son of a royal. He had many things to learn beyond the average child. More important, he must be protected at all costs. True, he had his own security detail, but beyond being proficient in protocol and decorum, his nanny should be able to defend him.

Yet even as she protested, she was not genuinely surprised. The other woman always struck Katrina as a tad uppity, as if handling potty duty was beneath her. But she tried not to judge. There were times when she wasn't too happy about doing potty duty, either.

"I am glad you understand," Julian stated. "I was wrong to blame you without knowing all the facts. That…is not like me."

"You have much to occupy you." With the apology, she found she could be gracious.

"Again you show your generous nature." He looked like he'd like to say more, but decided against it. His words turned quite formal as he continued. "I do not deserve your goodwill, but I will accept it. Along with my apology, please know you have my gratitude. Samson is lucky you were there to help him."

"It has been my honor." This time she spoke the truth. She would assist any child in distress, and these circumstances went beyond the norm.

In the midst of crisis she was happy to do her part. Plus Samson was special. He was a Royal Prince, a future leader of the world. Her actions reflected on her country and her Prince. It made her proud to have Prince Julian acknowledge she did well.

Suddenly lights started to flash through the room in a strobelike effect. Katrina jumped to her feet and looked out the window. The train had reached the Pasadonia Station. Unfortunately, the press had arrived before them.

Sammy came running and buried his face against her knees.

"Paparazzi," Julian snarled. "Vultures, all of them. Take Samson below."

She had already grabbed Sammy up and headed for the stairs. Neil met her at the top. "It is just the press," she told him. "I am taking him to the twin guest room. Can you make sure the blinds have been pulled down?"

"No." Julian spoke over her shoulder. "Use the master suite for him."

Confused, she looked up at him. "But—"

"He is the future of Kardana," he stated simply. "He requires the extra security the room provides."

Neil nodded an acknowledgment of the command and led the way below. He went ahead of Katrina into the master suite and made sure the window shades had been secured. While Neil collected Sammy's and her luggage, she took the toddler to the bathroom. Back in the main room Neil had returned. Julian had joined him.

The two men managed to shrink the room considerably with their sheer size. Their sheer presence. Yet they were nothing alike—one was a trained killer, the other a world leader. One lived life in the shadows, the other the limelight. Both were used to giving orders, but only one wielded power with the mere lift of an eyebrow.

And no one would confuse who was who.

Certainly not Katrina, who found it difficult to take her eyes off Julian. He stood, arms crossed over his chest, just inside the door. His amber gaze ran over her before he switched his attention to his head of security.

Feeling his gaze like a touch, she shivered. Luckily he'd turned before she gave herself away. She blamed the kiss. No matter how she tried, she couldn't forget the feel of his mouth on hers.

Did his lingering gaze mean he was remembering, too?

Putting the thought aside, she set Sammy down in the middle of the bed and moved forward to join the men.

Neil quickly took her and Julian through the changing of the master suite into a panic room. She carefully kept her distance during the process. She really needed to get her inappropriate attraction under control. When the lesson ended, the train was beginning to pull from the station leaving the paparazzi behind.

"Report," Neil ordered, obviously speaking to someone on the other end of his headset. "Beale, handle it," he directed, and then advised Julian, "A couple of men on the back stoop of the train, my lord. Most likely press. St. James reports no other suspicious activity. Please stay here while I assist Beale then make a sweep of the car just to be sure we have no other surprises."

Julian acknowledged his acceptance with a slight incline of his head. With a bow Neil exited the room.

"Relax, Miss Vicente. Knowing the mechanics of activating the panic room is just a precaution. We must be ever vigilant."

That was a relief. But the train picked up speed, drawing a question from Katrina. "How do you suppose Beale will handle it?"

Julian shrugged. "I expect he'll ask the unwelcome guests to disembark."

"But these trains get up to a speed of two hundred kilometers an hour." Her heart raced at the notion of debarking at such a speed.

"Occupational hazard. Something they should have considered before attempting to catch a ride."

"Your Highness!" At her shocked exclamation he gave her a tight smile.

"Do you imagine Beale throwing them from the train? No. If they refuse to leave while it is still safe, they will be restrained on the stoop and suffer a long, cold ride to the next station, where they will be charged for trespassing. We are not the monsters they are, Katrina."

"Of course not." She flushed because she had envisioned the exact scenario he outlined. To hide her reaction she strode over to the seating area and tried for a bit of grace as she sat.

Being around the palace since childhood, she well knew the press was anything but harmless. Rodrigo certainly proved just how far a paparazzo would go.

There was big profit in getting that money shot, a million euros or more, depending on how much skin or how scandalous the photo. That was the very reason she limited her assignments outside the palace. She more than most knew just how far a paparazzo would go for that money shot.

And this was not just any story. A missing Prince, an orphaned heir to the throne, these were stories of a lifetime.

Her nails dug grooves into the soft leather of her chair. Oh God, she should never have left the palace.

"Make no mistake." Julian warned her. "I have

no pity for the paparazzi. They are a relentless plague on society. Those men seek to prey on Samson's vulnerability, his moment of tragedy. I will protect him at all costs."

"I can see that." He'd already demonstrated the truth of his claim by putting Sammy's comfort and safety before his own on more than one occasion. Quite heroic of him actually.

Right. Her admiration for him was so not helping in her effort to fight her surprising attraction for the man.

"A single picture of Samson during this trip would set a photographer up for life. I will not allow him to be used in such a manner. Do not disappoint me in this matter, Katrina."

She glanced at Sammy, who'd fallen asleep on the big bed. So innocent, so dependent, so important. "You can trust him with me."

"I do." For a moment his brown gaze softened. "Or you would not be here. Goddaughter of Jean Claude or not." He gestured toward the bed. "Rest while you can."

Julian returned to the domed lounge, chose a large club chair. He leaned back and discovered the chair reclined. *Thank you, Jean Claude.* After a while Julian dozed but came awake when the train slowed. Neil appeared to advise him they were pulling into their first stop and they would be delayed while their car was transferred to a different line.

"St. James is posted outside Master Samson's room. I'll be escorting the trespassers inside, turning them over to the proper authorities." With Samson tucked safely away and their equipment confiscated, the men would be led through the car and delivered into the care of the French Transport Police.

Julian nodded his agreement. Once alone, he tried to make a few calls but was hindered by the limited mobile service. The third time his call was dropped he gave up and switched to text. He let his father know they were en route and gave his assistant instructions on several issues, including making arrangements for Katrina to have a room near Samson and the nursery. Once that was done, he used a digital remote to put a rugby game on. Unfortunately a bad glare on the screen sent him hunting up the control for the blinds.

"My lord." A middle-aged porter appeared. "May I be of assistance?"

Julian indicated the glare on the television. "I wish to close some of the blinds. Where are the controls?"

"They are here, sir." He opened a hidden panel on the half wall between the lounge and dining room. "Or you may use the controls on the remote." The porter approached and bowed slightly. "If I may, sir?"

He proceeded to show Julian what the digital remote controlled, which was everything from the telly and blinds, to the climate and fireplace. He could even activate the gate at the top of the stairs and summon staff, all without leaving his seat.

"Would you care for something to eat?" the porter asked.

"Not at this time." Julian thanked and dismissed the man.

With the shades at half-mast, the light in the room dimmed considerably, and before long Julian dozed again. Worry for his brother, for the kingdom, for Samson kept Julian from slipping into a full sleep. He prayed with all his heart for his brother's safe return.

To contemplate what must be done if the Prince and Princess perished felt like a betrayal of hope. But it must be done. Julian needed to be ready to make decisions and act as soon as his brother was found, dead or alive. Because the possibility existed that Donal would be found alive but grievously injured.

Plans whirled through Julian's head as he tried to anticipate every contingency. So much to think about, but as he slipped closer to sleep, his control over his mind slipped and thoughts of Ms. Vicente took over.

The look on her face when he intimated Beale would toss the pesky men of the press from the train had been priceless. How could she spend every day at the palace and remain so delightfully unaffected? In the middle of this hell he found her patience and generosity of spirit calming.

He had no business thinking about her, yet he never lost track of where she was.

Holding her in his arms last night had been a mistake. And not because she was a dear friend and royal Prince's goddaughter. No, it was because the feel of her had been burned into his memory. Her soft curves aligned perfectly with the hard contours of his body.

And the taste of her, all sweetness and honey, had seduced the sense right out of his head as he sank into the embrace. Who would have predicted she'd wake up and kiss him?

Though he was half-asleep, a frown formed as he remembered she'd thought him someone else. A former boyfriend.

Anger roused him as he awoke with one word roaring through his head. *Mine*.

CHAPTER FIVE

GIGGLES FLOATED DOWN the stairs. Katrina smiled at the sound. Sammy so deserved a break from the depression that had swallowed him these past few days.

She slipped through the gate, relatched it and followed the joyful noise to the domed lounge, where she found Sammy and his dignified Uncle Julian playing ball. Realizing the two hadn't heard her approach, she paused to watch.

Man and child sat on the floor, their legs spread wide, rolling a ball between them. Make that two balls. As she watched, Julian bent to the side and snagged a ball that had gotten away from him.

"'ou missed." Sammy laughed.

"Because you cheated," Julian informed him.

He'd discarded his jacket, rolled up the sleeves of his shirt and ditched his shoes. At first glance he looked as relaxed and carefree as the giggling boy. Only a closer examination revealed the worry and fatigue weighing on him.

He held up the ball. "Let's try this again. This

is your ball." He rolled it down to the boy. "And this is mine." He picked one up from between his long, silk-clad thighs. "You send yours to me while I send mine to you. You don't send them at the same time."

"More balls." Sammy hopped up and ran to the couch. He pulled out a drawer and found a ball twice the size of the baseball-sized balls they were currently using. He pushed the drawer nearly closed and plopped down in front of Julian.

Ball in hand, Sammy reared back as if preparing to throw the ball. She tensed, ready to intervene, but Julian pointed a finger at Sammy.

"What happens if you throw that ball?"

Sammy deflated a bit. "No play."

"That's right." Sammy subsided, and Julian didn't dwell on the near infraction. "You think you can beat me with three balls but I'm pretty fast. Prepare to lose."

"Go!" Sammy sent both balls rolling toward his uncle while Julian sent one his way. The balls went back and forth to the sound of Sammy's chatter until Julian pretended to fumble the two shot his way and they jumped the barricade of his long legs.

"I win!" Sammy shook his fists in the air.

Katrina grinned, enjoying the interaction. Then she bit her bottom lip, wondering if she should leave them to their play. When Sammy woke up forty-five minutes ago, he'd promptly made sure she was awake, too. After freshening them both up, she'd wandered out to the lounge, where she found Julian working on his computer. Not wanting to disturb the Prince, she turned Sammy around and headed for the stairs.

Julian had stopped her and offered to take the boy for a while to give her a break. She'd told him about the storage drawers full of toys and gratefully escaped. She used the time to do something totally for herself. She dug out a book, curled up in a chair and read for thirty minutes.

It looked like Sammy had enjoyed his time, too. To the extent that she really hesitated to interrupt his time with his uncle.

"Care to join us, Ms. Vicente?"

Julian's question ended her dilemma. She moved into the lounge, closing the toy drawer as she took a seat. "It is good to see you two getting along."

"Yes, it surprises me, as well." He sent her an arch glance.

Sammy popped to his feet and ran to her. He jabbered excitedly about his uncle and playing ball. She understood every two words or so. "What a good lad you are. I brought you some juice." She tucked him in the crook of the couch and handed him a drink pouch.

"That is your influence, not mine," she advised

Julian. Heart racing, she dared to address an issue of great concern to her. "Forgive me, my lord. It is obvious you are not at ease with children, yet you have worked to put Sammy at ease. I just wonder if there is any affection or if it is merely duty."

Julian slowly climbed to his feet. "You over-step yourself, Ms. Vicente."

The ice in his gaze nearly deterred her. But for Sammy she must persevere.

"Perhaps, but we spoke of Sammy having special needs in his care because he is a Prince, and this is true. But I feel it is also important to point out he is a child like any other and in need of love and affection."

"And you doubt the Cold Prince's ability to provide for him."

Oh dear, she'd hit a nerve.

"I have observed in high-profile families that structure, discipline and decorum often take precedent over emotional support when it comes to educating the children." She checked on Sammy, who sipped his juice. "I would not want that for Sammy."

"Samson," he corrected. "I survived such a childhood, Ms. Vicente," the Prince stated with cool reserve, turning to stare out the window at the passing scenery. "I can assure you my lessons in decorum and protocol have served me well through my entire life."

"Of course. I do understand the importance of such lessons." Oh yeah, she'd offended him. But Sammy deserved to have someone fight for him. Her time with him might be short, but she'd do what she could while she was here. "I just believe hugs and laughter offer balance to all the demands of his station."

"With any luck he won't have to suffer my clumsy attempts at affection much longer." The stiffness in his posture belied the levity of his words.

Her heart sank as his meaning struck her. She talked as if Sammy's parents were already gone. Shame on her for the appalling lack of tact. She'd allowed her concern for the boy to get the better of her.

"I am the clumsy one." She approached him slowly. "I have become fond of Sammy and I worry for him. But my timing is not so good. Have you heard any news of your brother and sister-in-law?"

"Nothing." She imagined the emotionless word held a world of pain.

"Oh, Julian, I am sorry. I have not given up hope for your brother and Helene. Truly. This is a bit of a soapbox for me. How duty takes precedence over affection. It is just so sad when I know it does not have to be so." Flustered over her faux pas, she let her mouth run ahead of her head. Yet as soon as she stopped, everything she'd just said reran in her head. "Now I am babbling when you are sad. What a puppy-head I am. And to make it worse I just called you Julian. I—"

He held up a hand. "Stop apologizing. A loss of hope is understandable. The crash, the cold, the distance—everything works against them."

He ran a finger over one dark eyebrow, the weary gesture a minute glimpse into his worry and despair. In the reflection of the glass she saw the anguish he kept so ruthlessly hidden. "Do not equate lack of affection with lack of emotion. I pray for Donal's safety while I prepare to take his place. Every directive, every word is the worst kind of betrayal."

Yet he was not allowed to let anyone see. His admission broke her heart.

Katrina checked on Sammy, found him lying on the floor playing with a dump truck and a racer. Satisfied he was occupied, she did the unpardonable. She touched a royal Prince without his consent.

"We shall pray together."

Warm fingers slid around Julian's hand. Shocked by the touch, by the comfort, he tightened his hold until he heard a gasp. Still, she made no attempt to pull away. Instead she squeezed back, answering his silent cry of need.

His gaze went first to her reflection, but it was not enough. Driven by a compulsion deeper than his will, he looked into violet eyes drowned in tears. He quickly turned back to the unseen view, undone by her unstinting compassion. He swallowed past a constriction in his throat.

Protocol dictated he rebuff and reprimand her.

He could do neither. The connection soothed him as little else could. Suddenly he understood what drew Sammy to her, and nothing would do but he stand silent and hold her hand as the train raced toward the answers he sought.

The helplessness and lack of news frayed his nerves. Rather he knew. Then he could do as he'd been trained and put emotion aside while he acted in the best interest of his country. Katrina might not approve, but there were times when duty served one better than affection.

"K'tina, I hungy." Too soon, Sammy wiggled his way between them.

Julian immediately and reluctantly released her. He felt her continued compassion in the weight of her gaze and the softness of her touch on his arm before she knelt down to meet Sammy eye to eye.

"I am hungry, too." She tapped the little boy on the nose. "Shall we see what cook has for lunch?"

His eyes lit up at the question. "I wanna cheese sanwiss."

Listening to their byplay, Julian pushed the button for the porter. A growl of his stomach made him aware of his own hunger.

The porter appeared. "How may I serve, my lord?"

"We should like lunch please." Julian ordered. "Has the chef anything prepared?"

"Grilled cheese sandwiches," the man announced without a blink. "Or a nice salmon steak with rice and steamed vegetables with a tomato bisque as a starter."

"Lovely." Katrina stood and looked down at Sammy. "Would you like soup with your sandwich?"

Sammy considered this, his nose wrinkling up as he contemplated the major decision. Finally he nodded. "I 'ike tomato soup."

"We'll start with the soup." Julian directed the porter, who bowed and went to advise the chef.

Katrina towed Sammy off to clean up for the meal, leaving Julian alone to pull himself together. He watched her disappear out of sight.

But unfortunately she did not leave his mind.

Young, smart, beautiful and impossibly idealistic, she was a very dangerous woman with her weapons of comfort and compassion. How easily she slid beneath his guard. She made him act against his nature at a time when he needed to be strong, be resolute. Another moment and he'd have kissed her.

Again.

Inexcusable. Yesterday it had at least been an accident.

He closed his eyes as he remembered the news that followed the incredible, unfortunate embrace. Katrina was Jean Claude's goddaughter. Taking advantage of her would not only be a betrayal of a friend, the insult might incite an international incident. Neither he nor Kardana could afford such at this time.

There would be no more intimate moments with Ms. Vicente.

Sammy came clambering up the stairs. Julian helped to seat him while studiously avoiding the nanny's regard. It was the way it must be.

Katrina absently pushed the salmon around her plate. He'd been remarkably kind after her earlier blunder. She'd felt so close to him for those few minutes they spent holding on to each other.

But in the time it took her and Sammy to wash up, Julian had distanced himself again. It shouldn't, but his coolness hurt. She knew better, of course. Any closeness between them was entirely in her imagination. He was a Prince. She had a shameful secret.

End of story.

Though she owed him one, she wouldn't embarrass him with another apology. No. She'd learned her lesson. It was best if she kept her distance. Reaching for her napkin, she wiped Sammy's face. From this point forward, her undivided attention went to the boy.

Twenty minutes into the tense meal, Neil appeared at the table with a satellite phone. "My lord, it is the French President."

For the space of a second Julian's gaze met hers. Then, stoic as a blank wall, he took the phone and moved into the lounge area. "*Bonjour, Monsieur le Président.*"

Katrina bit her lip, her attention switched from Julian's tense shoulders to little Sammy innocently eating his sandwich. If the president was calling, he must have news of Prince Donal. Sadly, Julian's posture did not hint at good news.

Heart going out to her charge, she gently ran her fingers through his soft hair. He grinned up at her then dropped the last of his sandwich on his plate.

"I done."

"Good boy." She wiped his mouth and handed him his lidded cup. "Now finish your milk."

He shook his head, his blond hair wisping about his face.

So not the time to press the issue. She stood and helped him from his seat. With a last look at Julian's broad back, she carried Sammy down to his room.

Katrina paced the master suite while her small charge lay on the bed and watched a movie on DVD. His eyes were already blinking and she knew he'd be asleep soon. Since his uncle's arrival, he'd really settled down and behaved rather marvelously.

Unfortunately, that was likely to end soon, as it did not appear as if the news Julian received was very encouraging. She wrung her hands, distraught on behalf of both child and man. What a devastating loss this would be for both of them.

She twisted the ring on her finger, feeling helpless as she waited to hear the exact nature of the news Julian received from the president. Yet the very fact it was the president calling seemed significant. She'd longed to stay, to be there for Julian, but the return of his reserve made such a move impossible. So she'd given him his privacy.

Equally as important was not letting Sammy overhear anything he shouldn't. They'd all learned that lesson. Too bad she wasn't as good at handling her own lessons, like the slight problem of remaining impartial.

Her mother showed concern when Katrina first told her she wanted to be a nanny at the palace. Of course she'd only been eight years old. Still, she remembered her mother's words at the time.

"You have such a soft heart…I'm afraid you will get hurt. A nanny must care but not become attached. You, my dear one, care too much."

To this day that was her biggest problem. Sammy had already wormed his way into her heart and, by extension, his uncle. But her mother was right; it wasn't her place to become emotionally attached. If she hadn't exactly learned that particular lesson, she more than learned the one where she refused to allow herself to be used.

She nearly pulled the ring off, twisted it back into place. The problem with her and Julian was they kept forgetting she was the nanny. Her by getting too attached, and him because he saw her as Jean Claude's goddaughter. The reappearance of his stoic manner indicated he'd come to his senses. Now it was her turn.

A knock sounded on the door. She rushed forward to find Neil standing in the narrow corridor. She shook off a stab of disappointment.

"His Highness would like to speak with you in the lounge," he announced.

"Is it bad news?" she whispered, anxious to know what was happening.

"I don't discuss crown business." His bland expression didn't change, but the sadness in his eyes said what he would not.

"Of course." She acknowledged his discretion and took it as a reminder this was not her household. Harsh, but now was the time to get a grip and start separating herself emotionally from Sammy. And his uncle. "Will you sit with Sammy? He shouldn't be any trouble. I expect him to fall asleep soon."

Neil agreed and stepped inside. Katrina wiped her hands over her hips and headed for the lounge.

Julian stood, hands clasped behind him staring out the window. She experienced a moment of déjà vu and slowed as she remembered her new resolve to keep her emotions out of the job. She stared past him to the view, which consisted of a lot of snow and a smattering of trees. She doubted very much he saw any of it.

"Your Highness." She stopped a respectable distance behind him.

He tensed at the sound of her voice, making his posture even more rigid, if such a thing were even possible.

"Donal and Helene are dead."

At the stark announcement she closed her eyes, fighting the burn of tears. Though expected, it still hurt to hear the news. But she quickly persevered and focused on Julian. The words held a harsh quality, sounding as if he'd swallowed a handful of granite.

"My condolences," she whispered. And then, because that seemed so inadequate, she added, "What can I do to help?"

"We will be stopping to collect the bodies before traveling on to Kardana. There will be a delay while we wait for them to be delivered off the mountain. It could take a couple days. Jean Claude has approved the use of the train car for the full journey. You should prepare for an overnight stay perhaps more."

"Of course, my lord." So clipped, so unemotional. Her fingernails dug into her palms with the effort to stay uninvolved. "Will there be anything else?"

He turned then and her breath caught in the back of her throat. The clenched line of his jaw, the sheen of despair in his golden eyes told of his struggle for composure. Here was a man who had lost his brother.

"Yes." He stood straight and proud before her. "I realize it is highly inappropriate to ask." He fixated on a spot over her shoulder, as if unable to meet her gaze. "You are, of course, at liberty to refuse."

His uncharacteristic hesitancy tore at her heart, drew her forward. "What can I do?"

His eyes met hers, and his Adam's apple worked as he swallowed hard. "Would you hold my hand for a minute?"

CHAPTER SIX

"Jul—ian." Her voice broke. Not hesitating, she went to him, wrapped both hands around his. He was cold, shaking. "I am so sorry."

"I didn't really believe it until now." His head bowed so his breath fanned over her cheek. "I knew the probability, but it wasn't real. My big brother is gone."

"He is in a better place," she offered, knowing it was too little, too mundane. She squeezed his hand, wished she could do more to ease his pain. No longer a Prince worried about duty, this was a man hurting for the loss of a dearly loved brother.

He shook his head less in denial than hopelessness. His forehead nearly touched hers, and she lifted a hand to his cheek and took the necessary half step to complete the connection, the comfort of skin to skin. A strangled noise came from his throat at the same time he clutched her to him.

"He's always been there for me. Such a bruiser, but he had the kindest heart. I don't want him to be gone."

"I know." She stroked his back; he shuddered under her palm. "You will always have him in your heart."

He didn't say anything more, just continued to hold her. She let him, holding him, too. So much stretched ahead of him. He'd been preparing for this—had felt guilty for doing so—but many would look to him now his brother was gone. Just as King Lowell had looked to his heir when he took sick last year. Those duties would now fall to Julian, as well. This time on the train might be his only opportunity to grieve in relative privacy.

Poor King Lowell. How awful to lose your son and heir. She could not imagine his sorrow, his grief. She'd seen him on the news yesterday talking of hope and staying strong while rescuers searched and the weather hampered efforts. Surely having Julian and Sammy home would bring him some measure of comfort.

Tears welled and overflowed, sliding down her cheek. She made no effort to stop them. Tightening her arms around Julian, she buried her face in his chest, allowing the fine silk of his shirt to absorb the wetness. In response, the arms that enfolded her were strong, and the cheek that rested against her temple held its own dampness.

"My father broke on the phone," he whispered.

"Just broke down and cried." She heard how his father's pain cut him deeply.

Okay, this was so not the way to achieve distance in their relationship. And she didn't care. His pain touched her. It would take a colder person than her to ignore his bid for comfort.

"It is okay for him to cry," she assured him in case the tears embarrassed him. "Even kings are allowed to mourn their sons."

"He would hate for anyone to know."

"His secret is safe with me." She backed up and gently cleaned his face with a tissue from her pocket. "Your secret is safe with me."

"How am I going to tell Sammy?" he demanded, voice raw.

"Wait," she suggested. "There is no need for him to know yet. Wait until he is home, surrounded by those he knows and loves in a familiar setting. I believe it would be less traumatic in those circumstances."

"Perhaps." He closed his eyes as if the weight of the decision took total concentration. "I am no good at these flash decisions. I like to gather my information, act from a position of knowledge."

"Making quick decisions is really no different. You just use the information you have. And then you gather more knowledge so you are better informed the next time you have to act."

"So wise." He kissed the back of her hand; the

heat of his breath tickling over her skin made her shiver, distracting her for a moment. The old-fashioned gesture was definitely not meant to be shared between employer and nanny. And then he turned her hand over and kissed the palm.

Her breath caught. Oh my.

He regained her attention when he framed her face in two large hands and lifted her gaze to his.

"Thank you." His thumbs feathered over her cheeks collecting the last of her tears. "You are a very giving woman."

"No one should be alone at such a time." She lifted her right hand and wrapped her fingers around one thick wrist, not knowing if she meant to hold him to her or pull him free.

"It's a dangerous trait." The thumb of the hand she held continued to caress her cheek, though he seemed almost unaware of the gesture.

"Why?" she breathed.

"Someone may take advantage of you."

A knot clenched her gut. Someone had. The harsh memory threatened to destroy the moment. She should step back, return to her duties. But she didn't. Because of the glint of vulnerability in his eyes.

Instead she bit her bottom lip and stayed put. For the first time she successfully stayed quiet. Perhaps because she needed this moment as much as he did.

"There is only you and me here." She blinked, noting the look in his eyes had changed. The pain lingered but awareness joined the grief. "Are you going to take advantage?"

"Yes." He lowered his head. "I am." And he pressed his mouth to hers. He ran his tongue along the seam of her lips then nipped her bottom lip. "You tempt me so when you torture this lip."

She opened her mouth to protest, but he took full advantage, sealing her mouth with his. Heat bloomed, senses taking over as sensation ignited passion. Large and warm, he dwarfed her, his strong body a shelter against the craziness of the past few days. He drew her closer, aligning her curves with his hard contours, taking the sensual escape to deeper levels.

For long moments she surrendered to his touch, to his heat, to his need. Lifting onto tiptoes, she looped her arms around his neck and got lost with him in a world without loss, without hurt, without protocol.

His thumb had found a new resting place, and her nipple peaked in response as a shot of raw craving ran through her. Too soon his hand shifted, moved down her side to the small of her back and lower. He cupped her derriere and lifted her off her feet. A trail of kisses led him to the curve of her neck. She arched into his hold.

Something vibrated against her thigh. A ring followed.

The real world beckoned.

Julian gently set her on her feet. But he stole a last kiss before he released her. He stepped back and pulled his phone from his pants pocket to check it.

She ran damp hands over her hips and took a step backward. She supposed it was something that he rejected the call.

She cleared her throat. "I should check on Sammy."

He nodded and crossed his hands behind his back in a formal pose. To remind himself of duty or to keep his hands to himself? "I suppose we're going to allocate this to comfort, as well."

"It would be best," she agreed, knowing as she did there'd be even less chance of forgetting these moments in his arms than their last embrace.

"Hardly logical." His eyebrows drew together.

"But for the best." She took another step back. "Do you not agree?"

He hesitated and then shook his head. "I'm not in a position to disagree."

What did that mean? Katrina stopped her retreat. Had the time in her arms meant more to him than a sensual escape?

But the moment was lost.

"You are right. It is best if we wait to tell Samson once we are home."

With that, he turned back to the window and lifted his phone.

The next two days were the worst of Julian's life. Waiting for his brother's body, and Helene's too, broke his patience. It took two days for them to be delivered off the mountain and be loaded into an attached cargo car.

His phone never stopped ringing. He accomplished much but recalled little of what he did. The weather improved enough that his assistant was able to fly down and join him, which helped tremendously.

Perhaps he should have flown Samson and Katrina on to Kardana, but he preferred to keep them with him. With his father's health issues, the raising of Samson fell to Julian now. It was right that the boy stay with him. That it kept Katrina close, too, was incidental. Or so he told himself.

That looking up and seeing her across the room calmed his frayed nerves had nothing to do with his decision. Nor did the memory of her kisses play any part in his decree. He'd be forever grateful for the comfort she gave him. He'd been hurting, and she got him past those horrible first moments.

To prevent Samson from being distressed, he'd

issued the order for no one to talk about his brother's passing. He kept all such discussions between him and his assistant for when they were working alone at the dining table upstairs in the dome.

"My lord—" the porter appeared next to the table "—you asked to be advised when we were within an hour of Kardana. We should reach the tunnel in an hour."

This would be the first time Julian had ridden a train through the twenty-three-mile rail and auto tunnel to the island of Kardana since the inaugural run.

"Thank you. Please advise Ms. Vicente."

"As you wish." He bowed and headed down the stairs.

Julian glanced at his assistant, Carl Brams, and met pale brown eyes through dark-rimmed glasses. Impeccable in a slate-gray suit, Carl didn't wait for instructions but reached for his mobile phone on the table.

"Security is already in place at the train station, but I'll alert them to our imminent arrival and ask them to advise his majesty. I'll also confirm the conveyance arrangements for transfer of the Prince and Princess."

"Remind them that Samson doesn't know. My father will want to see him. I do not want any slipups. This is too important."

As his assistant walked into the lounge area

to make his calls, Julian leaned back in his high-backed chair, away from the latest changes proposed for the initiative adding a police agency to Europol, the joint European law enforcement agency, which was currently investigative only. The vote would precede the International Peace Symposium in just under a month.

For the past few days his total focus revolved around collecting his family and returning home. But with that goal on the brink of reality, he realized how much he'd miss these days of quiet isolation.

Yes, he'd been connected to the world, and he'd stepped out to thank the French president for his assistance and expressed his gratitude to all those involved in the search and recovery operations. But for the most part this time on the train had given him an opportunity to mourn in private. More so than if he'd been at home.

A large part of that was due to the gentle solace of Samson's nanny. He purposely used the reminder of her position to aid in his constant battle to seek her out. Her quiet beauty and giving nature drew him like a bee to an apple blossom. Another time he may explore the potential of their heated embraces, but the chaos of his life made that a luxury he could ill afford.

Once they reached the palace, he expected to see little of her, something he both looked forward to and dreaded. Less temptation, but he'd miss their chats.

And the curve of her breasts in her prim, button-up shirts.

Plus the sweet sway of her derriere as she tended to Samson.

Heaven knew the taste of her already haunted him, and his arms felt empty without her in them. How could that be after such a short acquaintance? He could only hope the reverse would hold true, too, and out of sight would firmly put her out of his mind.

The plan held some flaws, as Julian intended to foster the growing relationship between him and Samson. The boy would need the extra care and attention after he learned of his parents' passing. To that end, Julian reluctantly made a note to address a replacement nanny for Samson as a top priority.

Carl returned to the table and time moved quickly from that point forward. Soon Julian exited the luxury train car and escorted Samson and his nanny through a storm of flashing lights and the thunder of hollered questions. The press swarmed the security barricades, aggressive in their demand for answers.

As prearranged, Julian paused to address the hungry mob of press. He stepped up to the microphone provided for the impromptu conference.

At his direction Carl continued onto the waiting limousine with Samson and Katrina. They'd managed to keep the news from the boy, and this was not how Julian wanted him to learn the truth.

"Kardana suffers a great loss as I return today with the remains of Donal and Helene Ettenburl, Prince and Princess of Kardana. My brother traveled to Pasadonia to attend a forum on ending world hunger. After the forum he and Helene decided to join a ski party on a jaunt to the Southern Alps. The storm that took much of Europe by surprise threw the plane off course and ultimately into the side of a mountain. There were no survivors. Prince Samson Alexander was left in the safety and care of the Prince and Princess of Pasadonia and returns with me today. An announcement of the funeral arrangements will be made soon. The royal family thanks you for your condolences and asks that you respect our request for privacy as we mourn for my brother and sister-in-law."

His statement made, Julian stepped away from the microphone. A barrage of questions followed his exit, and he happily left them for the press secretary. Within minutes he was sliding into the backseat of the limousine next to Katrina. Samson had been strapped into a car seat across from them next to Carl.

The fresh scent of apple blossoms drifted to

him as Katrina shifted to provide him with more room. He reached out to wrap a hand around her fingers, intent on holding her in place. Instead he pulled back and clenched his hand into a fist at his side. He'd just had this internal conversation. He was home. He could no longer allow the softness of her comfort.

"Look, Unca Julie." Samson pointed to something out the window. "That's by my house. K'tina, I home. Mama and Papa at home."

Julian met Katrina's gaze. His dismay was echoed in her violet eyes. He gave a slight shake of his head.

"Mama and Papa are not home yet. But you shall see your *grandpère*."

"The queen mother, Giselle, is also in residence." Carl informed the car.

"GiGi?" Samson asked tearfully, successfully distracted by mention of his great-grandmother. "She bing me a present?"

"I am sure she did." Julian flicked a glance at Carl, who pulled out his phone and began to text. Helped along by Katrina, Samson chatted on about favorite toys.

Julian turned his gaze to the window. Thoughts of the upcoming visit with his father occupied his mind. He hoped Father had found some peace in the past few days. Julian couldn't stand the thought of seeing his proud father broken. He feared witnessing it might destroy his own fortitude.

Katrina stared at her hand on the black leather seat, at the darker hand next to it but not touching her. Julian confused her. He obviously found comfort in her touch. A fact she took satisfaction in. It felt good knowing she was helping someone through a difficult time.

Yet now he held back. Which made her question, had it been her touch that soothed him, or just the warmth of human-to-human connection? She wished she knew, but it didn't really matter. The forced intimacy of the train trip was over. Best if they both retreated to their separate corners.

The royal Kardana palace was a fairy-tale castle set right in the middle of the capital city. Surrounded by beautiful garden grounds and made of brown stone, the huge house had turret-topped towers on both ends of the front of the manor. Gables and spires abounded and a broad two-tiered stone staircase led to a spiked gate.

Katrina craned her neck to see everything as the car turned into the curved drive leading to the main entrance. "It is beautiful," she breathed.

"It's home," Julian answered. He leaned toward her and lowered his voice. "We will encounter many people on our way through the palace. People may be upset and not watch what they say. Please take care as we go."

"I will do my best," she promised, but now they were here and the logistics came into play, it seemed delaying telling Sammy might not have been the best course to take. When she quietly mentioned her worry to Julian, he gave a half shrug.

"Too late to change things now. Between the two of us, we'll make sure it's okay."

Hearing him pair them as a team warmed her. She held the feeling to her as she followed Julian through the beautiful royal residence. She was awestruck by the museum quality antiques and art. She longed for time to linger and admire, to explore.

Thinking of Sammy, she stayed close to Julian. The staff they passed, nodded respectfully and showered sympathetic looks on Sammy, but no one mentioned his parents or the accident.

"K'tina, down please." He wiggled to be put down.

"Not yet, sweetie. First we need to see *grand-père*."

"My lord—" a portly man in a formal black suit met them in the grand hall "—his majesty and the queen mother are in the formal parlor."

He bowed and led the way to a door off a long hallway. He announced, "His Highnesses, Prince Julian and Prince Samson. And nanny, Ms. Vicente."

Carl stopped at the door, which made Katrina hesitate, but Grimes, the butler, gave her an encouraging nod, so she followed Julian's broad back through the opulent room. A mix of stunning antiques and modern comfort, the cream and burgundy room was both elegant and welcoming.

Lowell Ettenburl, King of Kardana, sat in a cream and gold high-backed chair. An imposing man with a full head of thick gray hair, his grief showed in the slump of broad shoulders and shadowed brown eyes.

"Julian." A sheen grew in his eyes, and he stood to embrace his remaining son.

The two men clung to each other and Katrina heard a few mumbled words. Her throat tightened as tears threatened. Finding the sight too profound to watch, she looked away, to give them privacy and to gather her composure.

She met the sad blue eyes of a grand dame. Dressed in a suit a shade darker than her eyes, she sat in a companion chair to the King. Short and a little plump, only her regal demeanor and rigid posture kept her from being swallowed by the thronelike seat. White hair wound around her head in an elaborate yet refined bun. Her lined face was made up to perfection. But the best cosmetics in the world could not hide the bone-deep sorrow as she watched her son and grandson.

"GiGi!" Sammy exclaimed. This time she had no hope of containing him as he practically jumped from her arms. He ran the short distance to his great-grandmother, climbed into her lap and wrapped his tiny arms around her neck.

The starch went out of the woman as she melted with love. She hugged Sammy so tight he protested and squirmed free of the embrace. But he sat in her lap and chatted away.

Katrina felt awkward standing there amidst the family in such a private moment of grief. The feeling magnified when Julian and the King moved a few feet away and began a hushed conversation.

"I rode on a train with K'tina," Sammy informed his great-grandmother. "I played ball with Unca Julie." Then, with total indignation, "Mama and Papa wen bye-bye and not come back!"

And while the room wheeled from that, he smiled with simple guile. "GiGi bring me present?"

Giselle blinked back tears as she hugged the boy to her again. "*Ja*, I always have a present for *Meingeliebterjunge*. It is in my room." Her beloved boy wiggled away and hopped to the floor. He grabbed her wrinkled hand and tugged. The queen mother patted the seat beside her, groping for a dainty handkerchief.

"Sammy, let GiGi rest now." Katrina took a quick step forward.

Sammy stared up at his great-grandmother before turning big eyes to Katrina. "Why GiGi sad?"

"She has missed you," she explained, keeping it simple. "Would you like me to take him?" she asked quietly.

"*Nein*, he is fine. I am comforted having him near." The older woman waved to a cream sofa. "Miss Vicente, please have a seat. You must forgive me…I am distracted."

"I understand." Katrina settled on the edge of her seat.

"*Oma,* forgive me." Julian bent and kissed his grandmother's cheek and then turned to include the King. "The fault is mine. *Vater, Oma,* this is Katrina Vicente from Pasadonia. She has been a great help with Samson's care."

Katrina immediately popped to her feet and curtsied to the King.

"Miss Vicente." He patted her hand then gestured for her to resume her seat as he reclaimed his. "Welcome. We thank you for your efforts on Samson's behalf."

"I am pleased to be of assistance. He is a delightful child."

"I spoke with Bernadette yesterday." Giselle dabbed at a lingering tear. "She described a situation that was less than delightful."

"Yes, well, Sammy was upset." He was the last one she blamed for any of this.

"Quite a shame, the fuss Tessa made." Giselle crossed her hands in her lap and tilted her chin up. "Such a disappointment."

Katrina said nothing to that. It wasn't her place.

"It matters not. We are home now." Julian took a place at the mantel. "And there is much to do."

Sammy sat quietly as he'd been taught, his little head moving with the conversation. His solemn expression worried her. He was taking everything in, but how much did he comprehend?

"Your Majesties, you have my deepest condolences." She purposely used a word Sammy wouldn't understand. "Princess Bernadette has released me to help for as long as you need me."

"Our Pasadonian friends have been very gracious. As have you, my dear," King Lowell said. "We have difficult days ahead of us and as you appear to have a calming effect on young Samson, we would appreciate your assistance while he adjusts to the news and we find a replacement for Tessa."

"Of course," Katrina agreed.

"Tessa go bye-bye," Sammy piped in, his brow furrowed. "Mama and Papa go bye-bye."

A look passed between the three royals.

"Ms. Vicente—" Julian offered her a hand up "—we need to take care of some family business with Samson. Grimes will give you a tour of the nursery and show you to your room."

"I understand." Everything inside Katrina rebelled. They were going to tell Sammy about his parents. And she'd been dismissed. She'd hoped to have more time to prepare him, though how do you really prepare for such news?

At the least she would have liked to be here for him.

Wasn't this why she'd come? To help him through the trauma? But no matter how close she'd gotten to Sammy, to Julian, these past few days, she wasn't family. Placing one foot in front of the other, she forced herself across the room.

"I wanna go with K'tina." It was a plaintive call.

She longed to answer the plea, to wrap him in her arms and buffer him from the coming confusion and pain.

The doors closed behind her.

CHAPTER SEVEN

FURY PROPELLED KATRINA through the palace halls. The in-house physician had sedated Sammy. Again. After being told the news his parents wouldn't be coming back, ever, he went into a screaming fit. The physician had been called and the boy sedated. She hadn't liked it then, but had understood to a small degree. Watching the boy's distress was not easy, knowing he was hurting saddened family and caregivers alike.

But there was no excuse, none, for continuing to dope the child. Not for two days.

Grief needed to be dealt with. Smothering it only delayed the process; it didn't relieve it. A point she intended to make to Julian who, according to the doctor, had authorized the prescribed regimen. She would already have voiced her opinion, but she hadn't seen him since the evening meal the day they arrived. And there'd been no opportunity for a private moment at that time.

She reached his office and addressed the pale, dark-haired woman with dark-rimmed glasses seated behind the desk. A nameplate listed her name as Marta. "I wish to see His Highness, Prince Julian."

"Nein." The woman didn't bother to look up from her computer. "His schedule is full."

Katrina gritted her teeth, knowing patience and courtesy would get her further than acrimony. "Carl—" The dark head shook again. "Then I wish to make an appointment with the Prince."

This earned her an exasperated examination ending in a scowl. *"Nein,"* Marta repeated dismissing her. "There is much demand on his time."

"I am here on a matter concerning Prince Samson," Katrina informed the woman as she gave her name. "It is of great importance."

Marta heaved a put-upon sigh. "Everything is of great importance," she muttered, and Katrina came to the conclusion this woman was used to working with Julian in his capacity as head of the treasury. A position, apparently, that required less decorum than Prince Regent. But she picked up the phone and called through to the inner sanctum.

After a brief exchange, she hung up and announced, "His Highness will come to the nursery to see you."

"When?"

Marta scowled. "When he can."

Katrina supposed that would have to do. She

thanked the woman and returned to the nursery. She paced as she watched over a very still Sammy. She'd already addressed her concern to the Queen Mother, but the older woman had faith in the elderly doctor. She made it clear she felt the sedation was easier on Sammy than the distress.

His listlessness scared Katrina.

"Sammy, time to wake up." She sat on the bed and gently ran her fingers through his hair. Hourly she tried to wake him. But he didn't stir. Hadn't stirred for the past three hours. She shook his shoulder and called his name louder. Nothing. Fear for him made her determined not to leave his side.

Just let the doctor try to give him another dose. The whole palace would hear her protests.

Her only hope was to persuade Julian of the danger of continuing to sedate the toddler.

An hour later she sat tapping her nails in the elegant nursery sitting room furnished in pale greens and yellows. No bright colors or playful pictures here. No toy boxes or riding horses. It was a beautiful room, but a sad nursery. With the door open onto the bedroom it allowed her to keep an eye on Sammy in supreme comfort.

Finally Julian strolled in followed by Neil. "Ms. Vicente, what is so urgent that it demands my presence?"

She surged to her feet. "Ju—Your Highness, thank you for coming. I am concerned for Sammy."

"Samson," he corrected as he moved deeper into the room. "We are in Kardana now. You must call him Samson."

She bit back a groan. Not exactly the sympathetic attitude she'd hoped for. "He is not yet three," she protested.

"He is a Prince." It was a bald statement of fact. One that did not invite argument.

If that's how he felt, he had the wrong girl for the job. All her frustration and fear exploded in a tirade. "He is a young boy who just lost his parents. He needs love and attention, understanding and patience, structure and routine."

Each word brought her one step closer to him until she invaded his space. She vaguely registered him signaling Neil, and the other man leaving the room. Mostly she focused on having her say.

"Now is not the time to lecture him on the burdens of the crown. Now is when he needs to be held and told he is loved."

"You called me here to tell Samson I love him?" His tone held the cutting edge of ice. "Do you have any idea what I'm dealing with right now? Funeral arrangements, press releases, the realignment of my duties, taking on the military, updating myself on world issues, the pending Europol vote. I'm a tad busy to be stopping by the nursery every five minutes to pamper a grieving child."

"So it is okay to drug him?" she tossed at him. "Just put him to sleep and your conscience is free for you to go about your duties?" Disappointed, she retreated a step. "After the time you spent together on the train, I expected better of you."

"Drugged?" He demanded. "What are you talking about?"

"I am talking about the doctor sedating Sammy. I am talking about the future king of Kardana being kept insensible to the point he cannot be awakened. Tell me, Prince Regent, how do you suppose the citizens of Kardana would react to such a picture?"

"You forget your place, Ms. Vicente." He walked past her to glance in at Sammy asleep in his bed. "You forget I saw the distress Samson went through before. Yes, I authorized the palace doctor to give him a mild sedative to ease him through the trauma. I was assured he would suffer no ill effects."

She crossed her arms over her chest, hugging herself as she paced over the floral antique carpet. Her ire calmed somewhat at his assurance. She had to remember she was speaking to a royal Prince.

"I am sorry, but see for yourself." She waved

him into the bedroom. "It is four in the afternoon
and he's been asleep for hours. I could barely
rouse him to eat lunch. He was lethargic and then
he went right back to sleep. It is not healthy. Some
sedatives are addictive. I am sure this is not something you want for Sammy, ah, Samson. The doctor—"

Julian's raised hand stopped her. The imperious
gesture raised her hackles, but he was doing as
she suggested and moving into the next room to
check on his nephew. She bit her lip and followed.

"Hey, Samson." Julian sat on the bed and ran
his hand over the boy's head. "Wake up."

As with her, there was no response. He tried
repeatedly to awaken Sammy, but got little more
than a drowsy protest. When Julian glanced at
her, she saw real concern in his honey-brown
eyes. "This is not good.

"Neil," he called as he lifted the child into his
arms. The security officer appeared in the doorway. "Bring Dr. Vogel to me. And have Grimes
bring me a change of clothes."

Neil bowed his head and disappeared. Katrina
saw the elbow of another agent as he took over
point on guarding Julian. She was surprised to
see such close security inside the palace and wondered if there was something he was dealing with
that he hadn't mentioned in his list of issues. But

seeing him carry Sammy into the bathroom distracted her from the random thought.

"Here, hold him." Julian handed the limp child to her.

"What are you doing?" She cradled Sammy to her as Julian removed his jacket and went to work on the buttons of his white silk shirt.

"We need to wake him up." He reached into the shower and turned on the water before stripping off his shirt and tossing it over the sink. His wallet went on the counter. The muscles in his broad back and arms flexed as he kicked off his shoes and removed his socks. He might be a numbers man, but he definitely kept in shape.

Catching on to Julian's plan, Katrina began to disrobe Sammy. The pants and underwear came off with a tug, a sign he'd lost weight over the past few days. The shirt was a tougher matter as it needed to go over his head and his deadweight made it difficult to maneuver.

"I've set it at cool not cold. I don't want to freeze the lad. If that doesn't work, I'll adjust it." Julian finished setting the temperature and turned to help. He yanked the shirt off, and gathering Sammy into his arms, he stepped into the tub under the full blast of the water. He was soaked in seconds.

Sammy startled when the first rush of spray hit him. And still it took him a few minutes to come completely awake and begin to struggle in his uncle's arms. Katrina used the time to gather towels. Julian hadn't closed the curtain, so she dropped one on the floor to absorb the splashing. The remaining three she kept on hand for the bathers.

"Let him get mad," she advised Julian. "The adrenaline will help fight the effects of the sedative."

He nodded, indicating he'd heard, but kept his attention focused on containing the slippery child.

Enthralled, Katrina watched. And what a sight. Saturated with water the heavy weight of Julian's trousers drooped down his hips to reveal the top of black knit briefs. Rivulets of water rolled over broad shoulders and down muscles bunching and flexing in his bid to keep the flailing Sammy from hurting himself. Or Julian. The boy had already landed a couple of good hits.

She supposed she should leave. Julian had the situation well in hand. Literally. But she was helpless to drag herself away. A wet, half-naked Prince Julian tempted her beyond good sense.

Besides the tub was slick; he could slip. Best she remain to catch him if he slipped. The visual of getting her hands on all that slick skin made her mouth water. She swallowed hard and began an internal lecture on the impropriety of lusting after her host and employer. Add in the royal factor, and it broke so many rules she lost count.

"Get a grip," she muttered.

"I have him." Julian shot her a glance over his shoulder. "But I now have a healthy respect for the term *greased pig*. Chasing them is a favorite event at our Harvest Festival each May. Do you suppose it's been long enough?"

"Yes." She leaned in and got misted with spray as she turned off the water.

Then she enveloped Sammy in a big white towel and took him from Julian. The boy shivered in her arms. She rubbed briskly over his little body and turned for the bedroom. She spotted the other towels and picked up one to offer Julian, but when she looked back, he was unzipping his pants.

He lifted one dark eyebrow.

Heat flooded her cheeks. She dropped the towel back on the counter and made a quick escape.

In the bedroom, she tugged a new shirt and pants from the wardrobe and dressed the irate child.

"Unca Julie stupid." Sammy announced.

"Uncle Julian was helping you." She corrected the boy. Her hands shook with relief at seeing him alert and talking. "You were asleep and would not wake up. Uncle Julian took you into the shower so the water would revive you."

He considered that while she put his right shoe on. "What *revive* mean?"

"It means wake up." A deep voice answered from the bathroom door. Julian stood there attired in a towel tucked low on his hips. "How you doing, lad?"

Sammy eyed his uncle. "You waked me up in the shower."

"Yes."

"Why was I sleeping a lot?"

"The doctor gave you some medicine," Katrina explained when Julian seemed at a loss for an answer. "But Uncle Julian is not going to let him give you the medicine anymore."

"It was bad medicine?"

"No, but medicine is different for everyone because everyone is different. You are little and Uncle Julian and I are bigger, so we can take something that may not work as well for you."

"Cause I little?"

"Yes." Good enough for the child's explanation anyway.

"Is that my present from GiGi?" He scrambled to his knees on the bed and pointed. A large gift bag with a smiling puppy on the front sat on a table inside the door to the sitting room.

"Yes," Julian confirmed. "You can open it if you like."

The boy was across the room in a shot, pulling a good-sized dump truck from a cloud of tissue. "A tuck!" He dropped to the floor and began to play.

Tears stung the back of her eyes. Distracted by the rude awakening in the shower and now the gift from his great-grandmother he was happily occupied, but he'd soon remember the loss of his parents.

And she would be there for him, she vowed silently. As heart-wrenching as his pain was to witness, she preferred it to the unresponsiveness of overmedication.

"Hey." Warm fingers wrapped around her hand. "He's okay."

"Yes." Rather than gape at Julian's naked chest, she looked down to where his large hand engulfed her smaller one. She'd missed his touch. The heat coming off him warmed her, and she felt the shaking ease. "I am sorry for the things I said, but seeing him so listless scared me."

"You were right to call me." He dropped her hand to run his fingers through his damp hair. "I should never have let it get to this point."

"You cannot be everywhere doing everything." She remembered his secretary's muttered comment about everything being of the utmost importance. Obviously there was a high demand for his time. "I know you are busy." She dared a glance through her lashes. "Every time I see you, I am apologizing for something new."

He lifted her chin on a finger until he looked into her eyes. Lowering his head, he kissed her softly, sipping at her lips until she longed to throw her arms around his neck and demand more. Instead he lifted his head and ran a finger along her cheek.

"And I always seem to be kissing you. We should both refrain from these activities." His gaze rested on Sammy. "No apology is necessary. I thank you for calling my attention to his condition. It is telling that he hadn't opened his gift yet."

A knock sounded and the door from the hall opened admitting Neil and a heavyset, older gentleman with an arrogant expression.

She started at the men's entrance and stepped back, creating a discreet distance between her and the Prince. Hopefully they would not consider it a guilty motion.

As he had earlier, the doctor gave Katrina a dismissive glance. "My Lord, how may I be of service? *Ja.* I see the child is awake. You wish me to give him another dose to make him sleep." He tapped the old-fashioned black leather bag he carried.

"No," Julian bit out. "I want you to pack your things. You are dismissed from your position."

"Your Highness, I do not understand," Dr. Vogel blustered. "What have I done to deserve this?"

"You recommended sedating Samson without advising me of the dangerous side effects. Plus, I authorized an original sedation after we told him and he was in a state of distress. I did not know you were continuing to medicate him."

"I thought to save him upset." The doctor defended his actions.

"Grieving is a natural part of the healing process," Katrina said. The man just rubbed her wrong.

He turned on her, causing her to flinch. She had the feeling he'd like to strike her.

"Quiet, upstart," he snarled. "It is not your place to speak now." To Julian he said, "Sire, you must not listen to this foreigner. She is not a trained medical professional, yet she tried to interfere in my treatment of the boy. I have served your family well for many years."

"Count yourself lucky she contacted me. I have been displeased with my father's progress. With this incident I am assured I am making the right decision." In nothing more than a towel, Julian projected total confidence. "Have your resignation delivered to me by five this afternoon. At five oh one, you'll be handed termination papers."

The pompous man's cheeks reddened, his outrage and anger escalated to such a degree Katrina worried for *his* health.

At the door, the doctor delivered a parting shot. "Prince Donal would never have treated me with such disrespect."

"No." Julian didn't miss a beat. "If he'd seen his son an hour ago, Donal would have killed you."

With nothing more to say, the man disappeared. At a nod from Julian, one of the security officers peeled away to follow the doctor.

"My Lord, your clothes." Grimes filled the empty doorway.

Julian looked down at his naked pecs as if surprised to remember he lacked clothes. She wished she could forget. His near nudity distracted her terribly. Wicked fantasies kept playing with her mind. Even as Dr. Vogel bellyached, she'd half wished the loosely knotted towel would drop.

With a last appreciative glance, she gathered up Sammy and moved him to the sitting room to give Julian some privacy.

A few minutes later, impeccably dressed once again, he came through the lounge to say goodbye to Sammy. She received a nod. "Ms. Vicente, I'll see you at supper."

And then he was gone.

Sammy came to show off his new truck. She smiled her approval and made appropriate truck sounds. He grinned and drove off humming, "Zoom, zoom."

Katrina stared at the closed door. Julian's formality felt cold, wrong. Yet necessary. She believed her father and Princess Bernadette would approve her actions regarding Sammy's condition. Not so much the kiss that followed.

Julian was right; they needed to refrain from such activities.

"What is this I hear about you cavorting with the nursemaid from Pasadonia?" King Lowell demanded when Julian answered his father's summons the next morning.

Julian sat down across from his father in his personal sitting room before responding. He shouldn't be surprised. His father had informants all over the palace, not least of which was Grimes.

"*Cavorting* infers a bit of fun. I can assure you there was nothing pleasant about the experience." He explained the circumstances, ending with his dismissal of Dr. Vogel. No need to mention the kiss. That was between him and the entirely too touchable Ms. Vicente.

"Was it necessary to get rid of the doctor?"

Lowell plucked at his robe. He hadn't felt up to assuming his duties for the day. Julian worried about his pallor.

"I felt so, yes. I requested referrals from the Royal Kardanian Hospital and have three interviews set up for this afternoon. I've given the times to your assistant. I'd like you to sit in."

Lowell frowned but waved his hand in an accenting manner. "Back to the matter of this girl. Julian, you are usually an exemplary model of decorum. Now is not the time to become lax in your duties. The world has their eyes on us. How we act now will be how we are perceived in the future. There can be no rumors surrounding our house."

"I am aware of that." Julian really did not need the lecture. He was mindful of the inappropriateness of his intimacies with Katrina. He fought off resentment as he resolved again to keep their encounters professional. "There is nothing between me and the nursemaid."

He frowned. It felt wrong to dismiss her as a mere employee. "However, I would like to invite her to sit with the family during the funeral."

"I hardly find that appropriate," his father protested with a scowl. "It would only add credence to the speculation already brewing."

"I disagree. Grandmother set the precedent of treating Kat—Ms. Vicente as a guest by inviting her to join us for meals. This would merely be an extension of that. It promises to be a long, hard day. Samson will do better having her there."

"She is a nobody. She cannot sit with the royal family."

Julian hesitated, knowing Katrina disliked using her association with Prince Jean Claude. He also knew she would not put her comfort before Samson's.

"She is not quite—" not at all "—a nobody. It may help you to know Katrina Vicente is a relative of Prince Jean Claude Carrère, and his goddaughter."

Lowell's head cocked at that news. "Really?" he asked in a tone of great interest. "She told you this?"

"Reluctantly. It is not something she plays on. Princess Bernadette confirmed it in a separate conversation. Apparently Jean Claude is quite fond of her."

"Very well, then. She may sit with the family. But I expect total decorum from you."

"Yes, sir." Julian bowed as he prepared to take his leave. He was happy to see a little color in his father's cheeks.

"Send in my valet. I may as well get dressed if I am to attend those interviews."

"Of course." Unsure of what put the fire under his father, Julian made his departure. Whatever it was, he was pleased by the effects.

CHAPTER EIGHT

LITTLE HAPPENED TO test Katrina's new resolve over the next week. Well, if you didn't count reoccurring fantasies of Julian haunting her shower.

She threw all her energies into caring for Sammy. His mood fluctuated wildly from hour to hour, tearful and missing his parents one moment, to quiet and preoccupied the next, with a few incidents of happy and playful.

She rarely saw Julian. Yes, he made an effort to visit Sammy every day. But the visits were spontaneous and never lasted long. And, of course, he gave his attention to Sammy. Which pleased her. Truly. She had no business wishing for more.

Anticipation pulsed through her as she dropped her gym bag on the bench of the women's shower room. She'd loved having access to the palace gym during her stay, and truly looked forward to her daily workout while Sammy napped. The time worked out well. At midmorning she generally had the gym to herself, which gave her full use of the equipment and the mat.

Today she heard someone pounding away in the main room as she changed into her gym gear. From the sound of it they were putting themselves through a punishing routine.

A few minutes later she pushed open the door and stepped into the main gym to find Julian—correction His Highness Prince Julian—in shirtsleeves and business slacks bloodying his knuckles on the punching bag.

"Oh my God." She glanced around as she rushed to the shelves against the wall and grabbed some gauze and tape but there was no sign of Neil or any of the security officers. Obviously Prince Julian had slipped his leash. A sure sign he'd prefer to be alone. A sentiment she could respect, except he was hurting himself.

She meant to tape his knuckles and then leave him to fight his demons.

"Your Highness." She approached him from the front and slightly to the side so he could see her.

He didn't look up, gave no sign he'd heard her.

She stepped closer, spoke louder. He rounded on her and she threw up a block.

He blinked her into focus. And all that anger centered on her. "Go away."

"I will," she assured him, keeping her tone brisk, following the example he'd set since their arrival in Kardana. With the exception of that one kiss. She held up the tape. "After I bind those hands up."

He turned back to the bag, started punching again. "Just leave."

"Your hands already look like hamburger."

"That was not a request, Ms. Vicente." It was a harsh dismissal.

"Of course, Your Highness." She nodded and moved away. Halfway across the mat she stopped. He'd given her an order, but she couldn't—just couldn't—leave him like this, both bruised and hurting.

She knew the cathartic value of a hard workout. She'd spent a lot of time in the gym when she lost her mother. At sixteen it was the only thing that kept her sane. But she managed to do it without damaging herself. Julian didn't realize what he was doing to himself. If he continued on, he might break a bone or two.

She swung around, planted her hands on her hips. "I cannot let you do this," she said hoping to get through his haze of fury. "Julian, please stop."

He didn't let up. "This has nothing to do with you. I told you to leave."

"You are angry. I understand. You have a perfect right to be upset."

He turned on her. "You don't understand squat!" His eyes were feral, his jaw clenched. "I didn't ask for any of this. I don't want to run the country."

"Okay."

"No, not okay." He raged. "I want my life back. The numbers. The quiet. The shadows."

"Yes." She well understood the appeal of the shadows. This was good. He was talking. Well, venting. Anger was a natural part of the grieving process. But he'd denied it until now. He'd been so controlled since he heard the news of Donal's death, so focused on doing his duty. The pressure had been building, a volcano ready to burst. No doubt his hands burned like lava.

"I don't know how to be a father." He paced away and back. "Sammy deserves better."

"There is no one better."

"Don't patronize me. My brother is dead."

"Feeling sorry for yourself will not bring him back."

Fury burned in his narrow-eyed glare. He dismissed her to return to the punching bag. "I told you to go."

"No." She saw he had no intention of stopping. She lifted her chin. "You want me to leave, make me."

He laughed, an ugly sound unlike anything she'd heard from him before. "Get out before you get hurt."

"I have a black belt in karate." She stepped

back, bowed, and then assumed a fighter's stance. Let him use his arms and legs for a while and give his knuckles a rest. "You will not hurt me."

His dark brows lowered. "I'm not going to fight you."

"Afraid a girl will put you on the mat? You should be." She challenged him with a palms-up wave. "Fight me."

He advanced on her. "I'll remove you myself."

He tried, but she blocked his every move, forcing him to fight her or back off. And he was too riled to back off. She suddenly found herself in full defense mode. He had skills, a mix of martial arts, and he was good. He made her work, but she was better.

She knew she could take him down. She just preferred he come to his senses rather than put him on his back. But she might have no choice. He kept coming. And he was strong. She'd lose her advantage if she let him tire her.

Time to go on the offense. Verbally and physically.

She put him on the defense, made him work. And when he was sweating, she talked to him, "It is not your fault. It is no one's fault."

"Sammy could have died. That would have been my fault."

Her heart broke at the pain in his voice. She should have known the medicating of Sammy would weigh on Julian, but he'd handled the incident so competently and Sammy was doing so well, she'd put it behind her. For Julian it had been one more thing already crowded onto his broad shoulders. No wonder the volcano finally blew.

Enough of this. She hooked his ankle with a quick kick and sent him sprawling on the mat. He caught her arm and took her with him. She landed on his solid chest.

"Ah, sorry." She tried to roll off him, but he held her in place. She stilled and looked down upon him. Anguish pinched his features, replacing the anger driving him.

"You saved him, Julian. Focus on that. Because I can promise you, it is not the last scary moment you will have. Children have a way of putting themselves in peril's way."

"*I* put him in peril."

Okay, this was just wrong. Julian had every right to his pain, even to his anger. Being beaten down by despair was another thing altogether. Bad for Julian. Worse for Kardana. Sympathy would only drag him further down the path of self-pity.

"*Oui.* You also put him in the shower. Get over it. The end result is what counts."

He rolled her off him. "Thanks for the sympathy."

"Sammy gets my sympathy." Thankful to be

free, she used the momentum to rotate onto her feet. "He has lost his parents."

"And I lost my brother." Julian climbed to his feet, turned his back to her. "I'll be glad when the funeral is over and we can get past this."

"Mourning Donal is not what bloodied your knuckles. Nothing so noble. This little tantrum is over the loss of your freedom. Your life has changed through no fault of your own, and you just want it to be done so you can get over it and move on." She flinched internally, being intentionally brusque didn't come easily to her. "What you do not realize is grief is not something you get over, it is something you get through."

Good gracious, next she'd be kicking defenseless little kittens. But sometimes you needed to be curt to be kind. She stomped to the door.

"You want to be alone, fine. Tape your own hands." She let the door swing closed behind her.

Just after three, Katrina strolled into the formal parlor holding Sammy's hand. In his other arm he clutched his new dump truck.

When the time came for her to leave Kardana—which may be sooner rather than later after the scene with Julian in the gym this morning—Katrina was adamant that she would leave Sammy with a firm foundation in his new family environment. She didn't know how it had been when his parents were there, but except for Julian's visits, Sammy had very little interaction with his immediate family.

Perhaps it was too painful for his grandfather and great-grandmother to see him in these first few days of mourning, and she respected that they were grieving. But Sammy needed them. And she honestly believed they needed Sammy.

Distraction and purpose were great alleviators of pain.

Under the circumstances, she decided to take Sammy to them. So she discreetly checked around and found out where the royal members of the household spent their time.

She learned King Lowell's regimen included a walk through the gardens most mornings, but today was not one of those times. But GiGi took tea in the formal parlor every day at three. So here they were.

"GiGi," Sammy cried out upon spying his great-grandmother. He ran forward, but stopped before he reached her and gave a very nice bow. "Thank you for my new truck."

"You are welcome, Samson." Giselle forced a smile, her deep pink lipstick stark against the pallor of her skin. She placed both hands in her lap; one held a lace-edged handkerchief. "What lovely manners you have today."

"We pracus," he advised her.

"Practiced." Katrina corrected. "He wanted to thank you for his gift. I hope you do not mind that we stopped by for a moment. Come along, Sammy."

"But I wanna biscuit," he protested, eyeing the goodies on the tea tray.

"We will request a snack when we get back to your rooms. We are disturbing *Oma*."

"Nonsense." The older woman waved her to a seat. "You will join me." She rang for an extra cup and some juice for Sammy before offering the boy a lemon biscuit. "Young man, let me see that truck."

He set the heavy toy in her lap.

"Oh my." She cringed slightly.

"Careful, Sammy," Katrina admonished him softly. "You have to be gentle with ladies."

"He's fine." Giselle ran a hand over his head. Color had come into her cheeks, and affection chased some of the sadness from her expression. "It is a fine truck."

"Look't this." Sammy demonstrated how the front scoop lifted toward the back. "And it's fast." He showed her that, too, while happily munching a biscuit.

A maid appeared with a second tea tray and the Queen Mother poured Katrina a cup of tea. Together they sipped while Sammy played.

"He appears to be doing well," Giselle observed after a few minutes. "I am happy for that."

"The distraction helps." Katrina settled her cup back in the saucer. "He is very fond of you."

"And the new truck." The wry comment was issued with a regal inclination of Giselle's gray head.

"Yes." Katrina laughed softly. "It is his favorite toy and has proved useful these past few days."

"I did not get it for him, you know. Someone else produced it."

"It does not matter. Regardless of who picked it out, it is your love that generated the gift. And he has taken great pleasure in it."

"It's kind of you to say so." She sent Katrina a sharp glance as she sipped from her fragile china cup. "I was concerned over the matter with Dr. Vogel. Quite distressed over his dismissal."

"I am sorry." Uh-oh. The visit was going so well, Katrina hated to see the benefit slide away because of her earlier actions. "Was he a friend?"

"Heavens no," Giselle denied with regal disdain. "The man is a bore. But he was familiar. And I believed he had our best interests in mind. But seeing Samson doing so well, I must wonder."

"The new pediatrician visited Sammy this morning. He seemed to like her. She saw no lingering effects from the sedation."

"Excellent. Please keep me advised."

"Of course." She set her cup on the table. "We should be going. I brought a book to read to Sammy in the garden. Thank you for allowing us to share your tea."

"You do not fool me, child." Giselle sent Katrina a shrewd glance as she gestured for the book. "I know when I am being manipulated. However, I recognize the good it does Samson. You may join me for tea tomorrow."

Katrina smiled and handed her the book.

Her walk through the gardens with the King proved equally as successful. When she happened across him, while pushing Sammy in his stroller, she saw grief weighed heavily on him, just as he leaned heavily on his cane. But seeing Sammy lifted his mood.

She asked if they might join him and before long she had him pushing the stroller and sharing memories of Donal and Julian playing knights and robbers about the lush grounds.

The stroller made him steadier on his feet, and they walked well past the time he usually allotted for his daily exercise. He told Sammy stories of his father while sharing some of the history of the palace. There was no mistaking the pride in his heritage.

Katrina finished the jaunt with promises Sammy would join him for his walk the next day.

* * *

Julian proved the hardest to pin down. Okay, she dragged her feet a little. But he did spend most of his time behind closed doors in his office. And he missed more meals than he made. Avoiding her? She finally resorted to joining him for breakfast at six so Sammy could start his day with his uncle.

She found him seated reading a newspaper on an east-facing terrace overlooking the expansive gardens. Dawn bloomed on the horizon and a chill lingered in the air.

A maid stood just inside the door. Katrina stopped. "Excuse me, Master Samson and I will be joining His Highness for breakfast."

"I will advise Grimes." She bobbed a curtsey.

Katrina smiled her thanks, swallowed hard and strolled out to the terrace. She saw the appeal of his chosen spot. It was a beautiful setting at a beautiful time. The deep navy of night gave way to a magenta edged with a rosy glow. Soon the sun would add a bright gold as the sky lightened. The garden reached clear to the terrace. Bougainvillea laced up the columns surrounding them, and newly bloomed rosebushes bordered the brick porch.

"Good morning." She greeted Julian with forced cheer. They had such a complex relationship. From moment to moment she never knew if he was going to kiss her or freeze her out. Today she just hoped for cordial.

He lowered one end of his paper and eyed her over the bend.

"Good morring, Unca Julie," Sammy echoed.

She ramped up her smile and childishly crossed her fingers as she ignored protocol to pull a chair out, seating first Sammy and then herself.

"Please, join me," he offered ruefully. But he did fold his newspaper and set it aside. "Good morning Samson. Ms. Vicente."

"My lord. I am being presumptuous, I know, and I did promise Bernadette I would be on my best behavior." She bit her lip a little over that confession. "But you are so busy and have made such a good effort to spend time with Sammy, I thought we should make some effort to come to you, too." She winced at the yellow bruising on his hands. "How are you?"

"Better than I have a right to be. The bandages came off yesterday. The doctor advises me I'm lucky I didn't break a few bones." He flexed his fingers. "That's because of you. I'm in your debt again."

"Not at all. We all need to vent occasionally." Not wanting to dwell on the incident in case he changed his mind, she changed the topic. "I see we have interrupted your reading."

"No. This—" he tapped the paper "—has become more habit than necessity these days. I now have advisors that present me with the news."

"You do not sound too pleased with the service."

"I like gathering my own information."

"Ah. And so you will." She glanced significantly at the paper. "Perhaps you will lose this need once you gain trust in your advisors. I imagine it will take time for everyone to work comfortably together."

"An excellent observation. You're very intuitive."

"No." A blush heated her cheeks under his focused attention. "Just a good listener."

"Yes," he mused. "I have noticed."

"What is giving you fits?" she asked, because obviously something was. "No need to give names or details. Generalities are sufficient."

He simply shook his head, his eyes never leaving her face. "You are a temptation, Ms. Vicente."

She bowed her head to avoid the intensity in his gaze. "I only mean to help."

"I can't deny I need help." Weariness flowed through his words. "Or someone to talk things through with. I wish my father were stronger."

"And perhaps he wishes he was needed more."

"Indeed?" His retort was sharp. "You know my father so well?"

"No, but we had a visit in the garden yesterday. I got the impression he sometimes feels useless."

"Quite the good listener," he observed. "That's ridiculous. He's the King."

"I know. But he is still human. And when we have been ill, we sometimes doubt our abilities. Once we let the reins slip away, it can be difficult to grasp them again."

"You're saying he wants to rule again but doesn't know how to regain his authority?" The notion clearly astounded him.

"Possibly. I hardly know for certain. I am just going on instinct. At the very least he might appreciate the distraction of a conversation."

"I hungry," Sammy announced.

"I am, too." Julian switched his gaze to the boy, and Katrina breathed again. "I'm having pancakes."

"Yeah. I wan' pancakes, too!" Sammy bounced in his seat. "K'tina wan pancakes?"

"Yes, pancakes and maybe some eggs and sausage."

"I wan' eggs and sausage," he demanded.

She laughed. "You want it all."

"I hungry." He nodded.

The maid appeared followed by a footman, both carrying trays they placed in the middle of the table. "May I make you a plate?"

"Thank you, Amy, we will serve ourselves," Julian responded.

"Allow me." Katrina began to lift lids and soon had full plates in front of everyone. Sammy glowed as he chomped on a pancake. He also had eggs and meat, along with some fresh berries. Julian had a much larger serving of the same. She stuck to eggs, sausage and a few berries.

Silence fell with the arrival of the food. Once a few bites were consumed, the quiet gave way to giggles as Julian teased Samson by trying to steal some of his berries. Katrina sat back and watched them have fun. Something she felt they both needed. These moments with his family really helped Sammy with his loss.

And from what he'd revealed, Julian would also benefit from a few minutes of levity. His phone rang, and she experienced a letdown, because truthfully, she enjoyed this time with the two of them. So much for applauding her own efforts.

But Julian surprised her by rejecting the call and responding with a text. For the next ten minutes he devoted himself to Sammy as they finished the meal. He talked to him like an equal, and Sammy responded well to him even when the topic turned serious.

"Samson, your Mama and Papa's funeral is tomorrow."

Sammy nodded solemnly. "K'tina told me. We are goin' say bye-bye to Mama and Papa."

"That's right." Julian wiped his hands and set the cloth napkin on the table. His gaze touched her before going back to the boy. "It will be a very long day. We want to say a proper good-bye, and the citizens of Kardana need to be able to say bye-bye, too."

"K'tina says lots of peoples loveded them." Sammy's bottom lip began to tremble. "But I loveded them most."

"Yes, we loved them best," Julian confirmed, reaching for the napkin he just discarded and wiping Sammy's cheeks. "You will have to be a big boy and sit still for a very long time."

"I be good," Sammy promised. "K'tina says I make Mama and Papa happy when I am good. She says they will smile at me from h'ven."

"She's right. Katrina is very smart." Julian threw her a thankful glance. "Come give me a hug."

Sammy hopped up and threw himself into his uncle's arm. He wrapped his little arms about Julian's neck and clung. Man and child comforting each other. She blinked back the sting of tears.

"Your Highness." A nursemaid named Inga stood at the end of the table. In her mid-twenties, the petite blonde showed sense and compassion the few times Katrina took Sammy to the nursery.

At her appearance, Julian kissed his nephew on the head and patted his back. "Sammy, Uncle Julian needs to talk to Katrina for a few minutes. Inga is here to take you back to your room, okay."

He looked ready to protest, but Inga stepped back and pointed to his tricycle. "I brought your bike, but you must be careful and stay close to me."

His eyes lit up. "Okay."

"Thank you, Inga." Julian nodded his dismissal.

Heart racing, Katrina watched Sammy ride away. What was this about? Was Inga her replacement? With the funeral tomorrow, was Julian thinking her services were no longer needed? She should be happy at the prospect of going home. Yet the thought made her stomach hurt.

"Katrina." Julian drew her attention away from the departing child.

"You are very good with him," she told him. "He still gets sad, but he is going to be fine."

"Yes. In large part due to you. *K'tina says,*" he mimicked. But he covered her hand with his. "I was surly earlier and I apologize. As you've guessed, I'm on edge. There are so many issues demanding my attention. I keep asking myself, what would Donal do? But the answer doesn't always feel right, and I end up arguing with myself."

"Julian, you must not do that to yourself." Unthinking, she turned her hand to thread her fingers with his. "Donal is gone. It is sad, but a fact nonetheless. Yes, he was well respected, but I urge you to follow your own way. You will not truly feel comfortable in the position until you do."

"You are probably right, but it is not as easily done as said. My advisors were his advisors, and they expect me to act as he would have. The Europol vote comes up soon and I'm being urged to approve the change as it has been presented. I agree with the primary purpose, but I have reservations about the execution of those changes."

"Then you must speak up," she urged him. "The advisors will adjust once you exert yourself. You are a highly intelligent man, a logical thinker. If you have reservations, others probably do, as well. And remember you have to live with your decision. If you do not speak up and the problems you foresee occur, how will you feel?"

He rubbed his eyebrow. "Not good."

"You wish to honor Donal, which is admirable, but how long will you act as his ambassador? Soon enough you will not know his opinion on issues and you will be forced to address the question or vote from your own perspective. You should just start now. Plus, who is to say Donal wouldn't have agreed with your position if you had discussed it with him? I believe the best way to impress your advisors is to be yourself."

"So wise. Am I supposed to tell them *K'tina says?*" he teased her.

She blushed. Blast her unruly tongue. But how did she hold back when he seemed so alone, so torn as he struggled to do right by his country and his brother. Since she'd already offered her unsolicited opinion, she added, "You are supposed to be true to yourself, to act on your own convictions. And talk to your father. You do not have to do this alone."

"Perhaps I'll do that. Thanks for the advice, but that is not why I asked to speak to you. The funeral is tomorrow. I want you to sit with the family."

Shock stole her voice, panic kicking her pulse into high gear. Never had she expected this possibility. Her palms grew clammy. To sit with the family would bring her to the attention of the press. Speculation would be rife and they wouldn't stop until they knew every detail of her life.

"No." She pushed her plate away. "It is a time for family. It would be inappropriate."

"I've already made the arrangements," he advised her as if she had no choice in the matter.

"Your father will not approve."

"I spoke with my father. He gave his approval."

"But no," she protested, "this is not right. I am not family."

"Katrina, it's okay. No need to get upset." He leaned in, cupped her hand in both of his.

Oh, she was in such trouble. His touch comforted and distressed her at the same time. She wasn't prepared for this moment. Had hoped never to have to tell him of her shame.

"I would rather not." She tried to dissuade him. "My presence will just provoke speculation when the focus should be on Donal and Helene. The whole country is mourning. They do not wish to see a stranger sitting with the royal family."

"It doesn't matter that you are not family. You are Jean Claude's goddaughter, a valued guest. People will understand. Sammy loves you. You, more than anyone, will be a comfort to him tomorrow."

Unfair. She'd do almost anything for the child, but appearing at the funeral with the young Prince would only bring more heartache down on the Ettenburl family, and they'd already suffered so much.

"It is best if I stay in the background," she insisted.

"He needs you." Julian was relentless in his persistence. He lifted her bowed head on one finger until she looked him in the eyes. "I need you."

"Oh Julian—" his image blurred as tears welled in her eyes "—I cannot."

'My dove, do not cry." His thumb swiped away an escaped tear. "Is this about the pictures?"

She froze, literarily went ice-cold. "You know?"

She couldn't look at him, couldn't think. How was it possible he knew about the pictures? Only a handful of people in the world knew. He was not one of them.

"Jean Claude told me before we left Pasadonia."

"Oh my God." She felt raw, exposed. Betrayed.

"He thought I should know of your concerns. It was an honorable move on his part."

"Honor?" She laughed harshly. The ugliness of the pictures flashed before her mind's eye. No wonder he felt free to kiss her. He thought she was easy.

"There is no honor in this matter. Everyone should have just let me stay home." She jumped to her feet. Home was exactly where she needed to go. "I am sorry you were made a part of my—" she swallowed hard "—unfortunate incident." She pushed her chair in, held tight to the finials. "I believe it is time for me to return to Pasadonia."

Pasadonia, but maybe not the palace. How could Jean Claude tell this man of her shame?

Had Bernadette known? Had her father? Her thumb went to her mother's ring, caressed the metal. She'd never felt so alone.

She stepped back, dipped into a curtsey. "By your leave, Your Highness." And then she fled. She didn't run, but moved with great purpose through the drawing room, down the halls, up the stairs to her room next to Sammy's suite. Happy to reach her refuge, she shoved the door closed.

And turned to find Julian looming large before her.

CHAPTER NINE

KATRINA BLINKED AT Julian. "How?"

"This is a sixteenth-century castle. There are many secret passageways throughout."

"So it is okay to invade my privacy?" She walked around him. "Please go away."

"No." He crowded her, forcing her farther into the room. "I'm sorry. I never meant to cause you pain."

"How could it not hurt?" She backed away from him, needing distance, needing to be alone to bind her wounds. "It was the most devastating time of my life. A stupid, shameful time."

"Katrina." He took a step forward. She took two back. He stopped, his expression anxious. "What happened?"

"You know." She wrapped her arms around herself to contain the pain, to hold back the tremors. Unable to look at him, she chose the ceiling instead. Such exquisite crown molding. "He told you. Just go. I am sorry for your loss, but I do not want you kissing me anymore. Despite what you think, I am not a loose woman. I will not be used in that way again."

"I don't think that." He sounded appalled. "How could I believe such a thing of you?" Now he sounded closer.

Damn him. He stood in front of her, too close, too solid, too concerned.

"You are the kindest, most giving woman I know. I think of you as smart, and intuitive, and gutsy. You're also sexy as hell, which is why I like kissing you." He cupped her cheek, rested his forehead on hers. "Jean Claude told me there was an incident in your past that resulted in some compromising photos being taken. He assured me all evidence of the documents has been purged, but you still fear they may reappear and cause an embarrassment. Now you tell me the rest."

"Is that not enough?" She tried to pull away, but he held her fast. With a sigh she gave up fighting. His heat, his strength were too much temptation. "It is best if I leave before the embarrassment can be visited on the House of Kardana."

"You're not going anywhere." His mouth moved across the skin of her cheek. At her ear, he whispered, "Tell me."

"I was young, stupid, naive. My junior year of university I met a man. He was so hot, so sophisticated. Totally out of my league. Yet he seemed to have eyes only for me. I should have known better, yet he flattered me, wooed me, fooled me. I thought I was in love, but he was a paparazzo intent on using me from the beginning."

"Bastard," he grated.

"Oh yeah. As soon as I started seeing him, he began hinting about visiting the palace. But I had a full load of courses, and maybe I sensed something was off deep down because I never took him. Thank goodness."

Julian drew her to the bed, sat beside her at the foot. "Where do the photos come in?"

She shook her head, and unthinkingly worked her mother's ring. "He drugged me—at a party—then took me back to my apartment, st-stripped me, and took some really ugly pictures. Some—" she drew in a steadying breath "—some of them included him doing things to me."

"Rape?" He choked out the question.

She closed her eyes, wished she could shut out the memories as easily. "The doctor said no."

He said nothing for several beats of her heart. She clenched her hands together in her lap waiting for his condemnation. He'd understand now why she should leave.

But he didn't push her away; he pulled her into his arms. "Tell me he is dead."

Bad, she was a bad, bad person, because his comment actually made her want to smile.

"When I woke up, the pictures were spread all around me. I was so sick, from the drugs, from the pictures. All I could think of was to call my dad. It was mortifying."

"And he advised Jean Claude."

"I begged him not to. But, of course, he had to. The Prince was very kind. I couldn't look him in the eye for months. But telling him was the smart thing to do. The extortionist didn't expect me to confess my shame so quickly, so they were able to capture him when he made his first demands."

"But he lives."

"Yes." She did smile this time. "In prison. For the rest of his life. Extorting a member of the royal family is considered treason in Pasadonia."

"Then he should be dead."

"So bloodthirsty," she chided him, burying her face against his neck, because deep down she felt vindicated by his reaction. "I admit at first I wanted him dead. He violated me. Not just my body, which was bad enough, but my life, my pride, my relationships, my future. He took it all from me."

"Not everything," Julian denied. "You fought back. You're a beautiful, courageous woman."

If only she believed him. "I am glad he lives. He destroyed my life. And I put him behind bars for the rest of his. My freedom for his—it is a fair trade."

"Katrina—" he lifted her face to stare into her eyes "—you don't need to fear him anymore. Jean Claude got rid of the pictures and all evidence of them. Do not give this psycho any more power over you. I want you with the royal family tomorrow."

"No." She shook her head, her shoulders, trying to get away from him. "This is the digital age. Nothing completely disappears anymore."

"Treason is a death sentence. If the man lives, he bargained the pictures for his life. You are safe from him. No one will ever see those photos."

"I am not worried about me." She stopped struggling to face him. "Do you not understand? I was the fool. I let that happen to me. If the pictures went public, I would be mortified. This is what I deserve. But it would not be me alone who suffers. The press would exploit my relationship with Jean Claude. Embarrassment to him, the Princess, my father, to you and your family is what I seek to avoid."

Oh lord, she hoped never to see such a look of defeat on her father's face ever again.

Julian kissed her.

He framed her face in his hands and took her mouth with his. His tongue breached the line of her lips and sank deep to tangle with hers. On a half sob she answered his demand, sinking into his arms. He felt and tasted familiar, safe.

But it was an illusion.

She pulled her mouth free. "Stop."

Safety was always an illusion.

"This is wrong." She struggled halfheartedly, but he rolled with her, pinning her back on the bed and pinioning both of her hands in one of his. His mouth went to the curve of her neck.

"What's wrong is your thinking." The breath from his words heated her skin. "You need a distraction to allow you to think clearly once again. You were a victim." He pulled the neckline of her yellow sweater back and licked her collarbone. "You deserve none of what happened to you."

"Julian, we cannot." She tried to reason with him when all she really wanted was for him to continue kissing her. "You have appointments."

"Today they wait for me."

She arched into his touch when his hand found the skin of her stomach and roamed up to cup a lace-covered breast. He meant to steal her thoughts and he succeeded. She couldn't think while his talented fingers worked her flesh. Could no longer remember why she wanted him to stop.

"Julian," she cried out.

"Shh, my dove." He levered up and over, releasing her in the process. He wiped tears from her face. "I would never hurt you." He kissed the corner of her right eye. "I'll stop if you truly want me to."

She looped her arms around his neck. "Do not stop! You make me forget when I am in your arms. You make me feel again."

"What of the boyfriend you thought me when you woke me with a kiss?"

She chewed her bottom lip, which earned her a soothing lick of his tongue. Had she once thought him cold?

"An aide to one of Jean Claude's ministers took an interest in me last year. He was attractive and nice. I thought I might…that enough time had passed. But I never made it past a few kisses."

He pulled back, watched her expression. "Tell me, Katrina, have I made you uncomfortable at any time?"

"No." Touched, she traced his jaw with her fingers. A little shy, she confessed, "There is no one but you when you hold me."

He liked that. "Then let us replace all the bad memories with good ones." His mouth settled on hers and his fingers went beneath the hem of her sweater to the button of her skirt.

"Wait." Her hands closed on his over the material. "Not everything. I—"

"Shh. No need to explain." He slowly worked at ridding her of her clothes, caressing and kissing her through the sensual striptease until she was down to her silky cream camisole. He made faster work of shedding his own clothes, and soon gathered her in his arms.

He made love to her with exquisite tenderness, worshipping her body from temple to toes. The softness of his touch teased, tormented, tantalized until she withered with want. She kissed his jaw, his neck, the ball of his shoulder, everywhere she could reach. She loved the feel of him, the taste of him, the freedom to come alive in his arms.

Sensation built with the brush of skin on skin, of muscles flexing, and hips rolling. Julian whispered his intentions and followed through like the true strategist he was. She thrilled to his every move, his exquisite care, his wicked demands.

"Julian," she cried out when he joined with her. And then rolled and put her on top, urging her to take her pleasure. She blinked, slowly grinned and wiggled to get her bearings.

"Have mercy," he groaned and cupped her bottom to help set her rhythm. And she reached new heights of sensation.

Taking him at his word, she moved, slowly, then faster, until sweat glistened on their skin and every breath was a gasp. "More," she demanded, biting his shoulder. "I want more."

"Then take more." Pulling her close he flipped them putting her under him. He reached new depths, drawing the passion tighter, the emotion higher. His kiss stole her breath, but she didn't care, only sensation mattered, only the race for ecstasy. And then he was there and taking her with him. She clung, body arched, and soared the exploding skies with him.

A short while later, when she'd almost caught her breath, Julian's cell phone rang in his pants pocket across the room.

Next to her he groaned.

She laughed and trailed her fingers down his truly magnificent back. "I thought I was hearing bells ring while we were making love." She lightly bit and then kissed his arm. "Turns out it was your phone. That is probably the tenth time it has rung."

"I'm going to burn the thing. Do me a favor and toss it in the fireplace."

"Right. And two seconds later your security detail would burst through the door. You know they are out there."

He lifted onto an elbow and met her eyes from mere inches away. "I know I don't want to leave you."

"I am fine." She kissed him softly. "Mission accomplished."

"Katrina —"

"Shh." She touched a finger to his lips. "I am fine."

"You'll sit with Sammy, with me, during the funeral?" he pressed.

"Yes. If you really wish me to. I will sit with you."

How could she abandon him, or Sammy, at such a vulnerable time? Much as she wanted to protect her secrets and keep her family from further embarrassment, she couldn't do it at the expense of an innocent child. But she would attend as Sammy's nursemaid. She must keep her association with the two totally professional. It was the only way to protect everyone she cared for.

The family met for breakfast the next morning. They ate in silence as the weight of the day loomed before them. Julian looked around the table.

His father wore a new suit, fitted to his leaner frame. He had a bit of color in his face from his walks the past few days. Julian worried about his stamina, but the proud jut of his chin boded well for his endurance. His Majesty the King of Kardana was a stubborn man of pride.

GiGi sat with a stiff posture and a pale complexion. Grief shadowed her eyes but was otherwise absent from her expression. She had experienced loss many times in her long life.

"Thank you, Ms. Vicente, for agreeing to sit

with Samson. It will be a long day for him." Lowell addressed Katrina.

"It is my honor, Your Majesty." She responded to the King, but her gaze met Julian's briefly before she went back to pushing eggs around her plate. "I am happy to help in any way I can."

"I also appreciate that you are joining us," GiGi added. "I hope I may call upon you if I need assistance."

"Of course." Katrina laid her hand over the older woman's. "Please let me know if you need anything."

Grimes came in then along with Julian's and his father's assistants, who began running through the day's schedule. The funeral procession would go from the palace to the cathedral two miles away where a full funeral mass would be performed for family and invited friends and dignitaries. The procession would then move on to the National Cemetery, and Prince Donal and Princess Helene would be laid to rest. Afterward, a grand reception would be hosted at the palace.

Julian watched Katrina while the day's obligations were outlined. He'd thought much on her revelations the day before. Truthfully, it preyed on his mind. She was so giving, so courageous, she deserved better than to live in fear of an eventuality that would never occur.

Since Donal's passing so much of what Julian

dealt with daily was reactive. He hadn't had a chance to get ahead of anything yet. And it chafed against his nature. She urged him to give it time. And so he would.

How he wished he'd met her at another time. Any other time.

The situation was just so difficult. He needed the comfort she offered, the gift of her passion, a gift beyond measure. Which tore him asunder, because being with her, no matter how brilliant it was, directly defied his father's decree to leave her alone.

He wasn't a rebel, never had been. But today he chose Katrina.

At the church, King Lowell escorted his mother to the front pew. Katrina followed behind, carrying Samson. Julian acted as pallbearer for Donal and then joined the family, sitting between GiGi and Samson.

A hint of apples reached him giving him a much-needed boost. Inhaling deeply he took great solace in having Katrina close by. He glanced over at her. She wore a severe sheath dress in unrelieved black. Her intent, he knew, was to downplay her appearance in the hopes of fading into the background. A corner of his mouth ticked up. Her pale skin and vibrant red hair made that impossible.

He checked on Sammy. He sat quietly with

Katrina's hand resting over his on his leg. The unity between them was a beautiful thing. Julian reached out and placed his hand over hers and Sammy's. Immediately the peace of that unity swelled to include him.

He gave the eulogy, a task more difficult than he'd anticipated. When he regained his seat, Sammy looked at him with solemn eyes and climbed into his arms to rest his head on Julian's shoulder. He welcomed the human contact. The boy had been remarkably well behaved. Julian credited Katrina's presence for that.

Even as he had the thought, she reached over and patted the boy on the back. Sammy sighed and closed his eyes. Julian expected he'd soon fall asleep. To show his thanks for her support he covered her hand with his, lacing their fingers.

She frowned and tried to pull free. He held firm as he turned his attention to the Minister of Defense, who was praising Donal's military career. Helene's father and a friend honored her memory with a few words. And then the service ended and it was time to move to the cemetery.

When he stood, Julian retained hold of Katrina's hand. She immediately shifted so her body hid the contact and discreetly, yet firmly, yanked her hand from his.

"Behave," she whispered.

He turned and passed a sleeping Sammy to her. "We have nothing to hide."

"Julian—I mean, Your Highness, please stop."

"My dove—" he ran his hand over Sammy's back, but he held her gaze captive "—if you call me Your Highness again, I will kiss you in front of everyone here. I don't do pretense well. Today is not the day for me to try."

"I prefer not to draw attention," she reminded him, insistent in her gentle way.

"Just so. I must attend my role as pallbearer." With a squeeze of her elbow he stepped out of the pew and took his place at the head of his brother's casket. *Soon, brother*, he thought, *you will be at rest. Be at peace. I will watch over Samson.*

"My dear Katrina." At the reception Princess Bernadette flowed up and kissed Katrina on the cheek. "You do us proud. And this little one, what a good boy you are." She caressed Sammy's cheek.

"Bernadette." Katrina relaxed for the first time in a very tense day. "I did not know you were coming."

"Of course we came. Donal and Helene were friends." She gracefully sank into a chair against the wall and Katrina took the seat next to her.

A waiter immediately appeared with a tray of wine. Bernadette took a glass but Katrina shook her head. Sammy squirmed around in her lap and rested his head on her chest. She looked down to see his eyes closing.

"But I thought Jean Claude was scheduled to visit Canada."

"For a presentation on health care," Bernadette confirmed. "He delayed the trip to attend the funeral, but he speaks tomorrow. We will have to leave soon. I have only a few minutes before he comes for me. Tell me how you are doing."

Terrible. I have fallen in love with my employer, a royal Prince and future world leader. Katrina longed to share her dilemma with her friend and mentor, but now was not the time. Plus Bernadette would encourage her to pursue her feelings when clearly Katrina could not risk the association.

"The Ettenburls have been very kind and welcoming."

"Julian has sung your praises to Jean Claude." Bernadette eyed Katrina over her wineglass. "He sounds quite smitten."

"Do not tease."

"I am not. Believe me, dear, it is not like Julian to enthuse over much."

Katrina's heart rejoiced at the other woman's words, but she remembered the need for decorum, which meant keeping her relationship with the

Prince strictly professional. "He is simply grateful for my help with Sammy."

Bernadette's alert green gaze swept over the room. "I'm glad we are not staying long. Tragedy is a great equalizer, but too many world leaders in one place is a dangerous temptation."

"Julian has great respect for Jean Claude. I know he will appreciate that you came."

"Hmm. Julian." The sparkling emerald gaze landed on her face. "You are not as indifferent as you would like me to believe."

Indifferent? No. In trouble, oh yeah. She was in way over her head. She couldn't breathe without thinking of the stolen moments in her bed yesterday. Sitting beside him in church and at the cemetery, smelling the yummy scent of man and soap, knowing he was hurting and being unable to touch him had been torture.

She eyed his broad-shouldered frame across the room. Expression somber, he nodded and talked, accepted condolences and moved from person to person, group to group. No one would guess how he hated this. How he yearned for it all to be over.

"You love him," Bernadette said softly.

Katrina cringed. "Am I so easy to read?"

"Yes." Bernadette leaned close. "It is part of your charm. I am so happy for you."

"Nothing can come of it." Katrina shook her head.

"He does not return your affections?"

"Yes." Flustered, she thought first of his passion, but he had not talked of his feelings. "No. I do not know. That is not the point."

"I would argue that is entirely the point. I know you, Katrina. This is about the pictures. You must put your fears aside. The pictures have been destroyed."

She bowed her head. "I know."

"But you do not believe. Do you think Jean Claude would lie to you about such a thing? That I would?"

"No." She lifted contrite eyes to her friend's face. "Of course not. But I fear there is no way of knowing for sure."

"There is faith. There is trusting in those who love you."

"It is for them I fear. I will not be responsible for bringing shame to my family again. I will most assuredly not add another royal family to the list of victims."

"You are not responsible. No one blames you. All your family wants is for you to be happy. You were always so fearless. Grab some of that old energy and go after what you want."

"Bernadette!" Katrina protested.

"You need a man you can trust, and he needs

some warmth in his life." Bernadette bumped shoulders with Katrina. "It is the perfect match."

"I am here to help. Not for romance."

"My dear—" Bernadette ran her hand over the sleeping boy's fine hair "—romance chooses its own time."

Katrina smothered a yawn as she circled the buffet table. Today started early and dragged minute by millisecond. Sammy, bless him, had been a perfect angel. Of course he didn't understand much of what went on, only that they were saying goodbye to his parents. Even at such a tender age, he knew his role as Prince demanded a stoic public image.

She'd taken him to his room after saying goodbye to Bernadette and Jean Claude.

"Where is Sammy?" Julian appeared beside her.

"There you are," she said. "I was looking for you. Have you had anything to eat?"

He shook his head. "I haven't had two seconds to myself. Samson?"

"I just came from putting him to bed. I will not lie. I was tempted to escape to my room." She didn't admit he was the reason she'd braved the crowd. He looked great in his designer suit, so regal. But he'd lost weight in the past week, and she saw the fatigue he tried hard to disguise.

"No one would blame you." He curled a lock of her hair around his index finger. "I sent GiGi off to her rooms. Father insists on staying to the end. He's seated at the head of the room with Grimes stationed nearby. He'll advise me if my father begins to flag."

"It sounds like you have taken care of everyone but yourself." She handed him her plate and reached for a new one to fill up for her. And to put her out of his reach.

He'd become very touchy-feely today. His behavior threw her. She relished the intimacy at the same time she must reject it. Every touch, every nearness was noted. By the family, by visiting friends and dignitaries, by the staff. And worst of all, by the few members of the press admitted to the reception.

His attention seriously damaged her efforts to stay in the background.

"I'm not hungry." He belied his claim by eating a piece of ham. "I just want this day to be over."

"You gave a beautiful eulogy, *très* heartfelt."

"It was not difficult. My brother was a great man." He nodded at the British Prime Minister as he directed her with a hand in the small of her back to a table for two just outside the open terrace doors.

"Perhaps we should join another table," she suggested pointedly.

"No." He pulled out a chair for her.

"You are drawing undo attention to us."

"I wish for a few minutes' peace." She heard the weariness in his voice. "A few minutes when I do not have to make conversation, or accept condolences, or dodge ill-disguised political posturing. I can only get that with you. Is that so much to ask?"

Her lower lip suffered her indecision. This was not a good idea. But how could she deny him when she saw his need. When she longed to spend time with him, too.

"I suppose a few minutes could not hurt." She slipped onto the chair he held. "We are out of the way out here." Dusk loomed on the horizon washing the terrace in shadows. The scent of roses drifted on the cool spring air.

"Exactly so." His seat put him deep in a corner, somewhat obscuring his features.

She relaxed a little. "I will stay as long as you eat."

He sighed. "You drive a hard bargain." But he reached for his fork. The first two bites were to appease her, but then he really dug in.

With a small smile she picked up her fork. The quiet of the patio soothed her disquiet. Breakfast had been a long time ago, and she'd been too nervous to eat much. The food was delicious. The ham had a savory smokiness complimented by the fresh fruit and salad she tried, but it was the chocolate trifle that had her humming her approval.

"You must try this." She held out a bite, and he leaned forward to accept the decadent offering.

"Cook's trifle." He declared. "One of my favorites."

She pushed her plate into the middle of the table and they shared the remainder of the dessert.

"Thank you." He laid his hand over hers on the table. "I needed this."

Yes, he had. But a half hour of semi privacy merely teased. Seeing him relax only to tense whenever anyone came close to the terrace door or stepped out onto the terrace further along made her feel guilty for trying to deny him.

"You need more time." She flipped her hand under his. "After this is over, you should escape for a while. Just take off for the night."

"Lord, that's a great idea." His eyes lit up at the prospect of getting away. "I'll make the arrangements. Be ready at eight."

"Oh, but I—"

"You are brilliant." He lifted her hand to his mouth and kissed her palm. "I was wondering how I would make it through the end of the event, but knowing escape is near, I can handle anything."

"Julian." She pulled her hand away determined to disabuse him of his assumption. "I cannot—"

"Julian," a female voice interrupted.

Katrina looked up to find Tessa stepping up to their table. Katrina tucked her hands into her lap, but the lift of a dark eyebrow indicated Tessa had noticed her holding hands with the Prince. She received no other acknowledgment.

"Tessa." Julian politely rose to his feet to greet Samson's former nanny. "Thank you for coming to the services. Helene would be happy to know you were here."

"She was my friend. Of course I came." The woman tugged on the hem of her jacket, drawing attention to the way the designer suit flattered her slim curves. "I was hoping I might have a private moment with you."

Before he could refuse, Katrina stood. "I will check on your father."

"This will only take a moment," he objected.

"Take your time." She gathered their used plates and deposited them on a tray inside the door. A glance around revealed no one seemed to be showing any extra interest in her reappearance. Good. Hopefully that meant her *tête-à-tête* with Julian may have gone unnoticed.

Trying not to obsess about his conversation with Tessa, Katrina wove her way through the dwindling crowd to where Lowell sat at the head of the room surrounded by well-wishers. She sidled up to Grimes.

"How is he doing?"

"He is tiring."

Weren't they all? And now she had to worry over Julian's plan to escape. Yes, he needed the break, but it was insane for her to go with him.

"Has he eaten?"

"He says he is not hungry."

"Hmm." Like father like son. "If you make him up a plate, I will get it to him."

"I will see to it, *Fräulein*." He disappeared without a sound, a neat trick on the marble flooring. With his exit, she assumed his duty of keeping tabs on the King. The man was as stubborn as his son.

Thoughts of Julian drew her gaze to the terrace door she just entered in time to watch Tessa come storming inside. Oops, it appeared the conversation hadn't gone as she hoped. On her heels came Julian. He headed toward the front of the room, but was immediately surrounded and detained. It would take him a while to make it to his father's side.

"*Fräulein*." Grimes returned carrying a tray of food and drink.

"Give me a minute and then bring the tray over. Can you stand interference while he eats?"

"Child—" he gave a haughty nod "—I have done so for thirty years."

She realized the longtime steward must also be mourning. She gave his arm a small squeeze. "The family is lucky to have you."

Braving the crowd monopolizing the monarch, she loudly cleared her throat. "Excuse me, Your Highness," she said into the sudden silence. "May I have a word? It is regarding Master Samson."

"Of course." Lowell waved her forward. Happy with the success of her ploy, she moved to his side. She didn't expect him to make introductions. "It was very thoughtful of Jean Claude and Princess Bernadette to come to the services. It is a shame they could not stay long. But they are well represented by this young lady. Katrina Vicente is Jean Claude's goddaughter. She has been a treasure assisting with Samson, who understandably has had a difficult time adjusting."

She flushed as murmurs of approval echoed around her. She forced a conciliatory smile. "If you would give us a few minutes?"

To her relief, people melted back into the throng of visitors leaving her and the King alone.

King Lowell heaved a weary sigh. "My dear, what is this about Samson?"

"He is sleeping, lucky boy." She waved to Grimes. "He conked out after a bit of supper.

Speaking of food, I asked Grimes to get a plate for me. Do you mind if I eat while we talk?"

"Be at ease, my child." He gave his approval as the tray was set on a table between them. Grimes took up sentinel duty a few feet away.

"Oh my—" Katrina deliberately overplayed her part "—so much food, you will have to help me eat some of this."

King Lowell glanced from the food to Grimes's back. "I see. I have been set up. There is no issue regarding Samson."

"Not true." She held the plate up to tempt him. "He will be quite upset if you are too tired to walk in the garden with him tomorrow."

"Perhaps I will have a bite." He reached for a piece of roast beef. "We wouldn't want to disappoint the child."

"No," she agreed.

"You are a bit of a meddler, are you not *fräulein*?"

"I prefer to think of it as caring."

"I imagine you do. You can be quite subtle. But not tonight."

"You do not fool easily." She stole a berry from the plate. "And this is more entertaining. You looked like you could use a perking up."

"Hmm." He hummed his agreement. "It would appear you have us Kardanians wrapped around your finger."

"Hardly, Your Majesty." She gave a delicate snort. "You are a headstrong lot."

He laughed. "Just so. Ah, here comes Julian. I wonder if he has spoken with Tessa. When we spoke, she indicated she'd be interested in returning as Samson's nanny. I believe he would benefit from having someone familiar, don't you?"

CHAPTER TEN

"I ALWAYS THOUGHT of secret passages as being dark and creepy with dust and spiderwebs throughout." Katrina followed Julian's broad back through a narrow hallway. "This is well lit and tidy." She sniffed. "Are these walls cedar?"

"I have no idea. Donal and Helene used this passage to get to the nursery from their rooms. It's faster and more direct than taking the corridors. The servants also use them in matters of urgency."

"Convenient."

He glanced at her over his shoulder. "I recently had them clean the passages from my rooms to the nursery."

"Really?" Why had he felt the need to do so?

"*Ja*. After the episode with Dr. Vogel, I like to check on Sammy on my way to bed at night."

"Just Sammy?"

Julian stopped and turned to her. "Yes, my dove." He ran his thumb over the dent in her chin. "Yesterday was the first time I used the tunnel to access your room. I'm actually quite a decent chap."

"You—" she jabbed him in the chest "—are a blackguard of the highest order, sneaking me out of the palace."

"It was your idea." He kissed her briefly and resumed their trek through the inner labyrinth of the castle.

"I suggested you escape for the night. I was not proposing a lover's tryst."

"But this is so much better."

"You would think so, considering it is your idea. I really should have argued more. It was a tough day for Sammy." She fretted. "He may well have a restless night."

"We checked on him. He was out like a light." He led her down three flights of stairs and opened the door at the bottom. Fresh air wafted inside revealing the door opened to the outdoors.

This was her last chance to change her mind. To act with rationality and wisdom.

Her heart raced as he turned off the light and opened the door wider to look out. He grinned at her. And that's all it took. Stealing his excitement and joy was beyond her. She threw caution to the cool breeze streaming through the door.

Blood pumped wild and fast through her veins as adrenaline spiked. She hadn't felt this alive in years. She wanted this adventure. She wanted him. Craved time alone to explore the passion between them.

Bernadette had challenged Katrina to find her spine and go after what she wanted. She wasn't so selfish she'd risk a public relationship with him. But she could have tonight. A passionate gem to add to her memories before it was time to return home.

"The garage is just across the courtyard. My car is fueled and waiting. Neil knows we're going and has notified a guard at the gate that you are using my auto to drive an unwell guest home."

"You want me to drive?"

"Ja."

"Your car?" she clarified.

"Ja." His eyes narrowed in suspicion. "You can drive stick, yes?"

"Oui." She rubbed her hands together. "Let us go."

The moonlight showed the corner of his mouth notch up. "You do not wish to change your mind? Someone may see us and raise the alarm."

Her body was singing now. "Tease," she mocked him. "You would not let me change my mind."

"No," he agreed. His mouth claimed hers, searing her with a heated kiss. "Tonight you belong to me."

When he released her, she blinked up at him.

She licked her lips, tasting him, drew in a deep breath that filled her with his scent. And gave a wiggle to make sure the strength had returned to her legs.

"What are we waiting for?" she asked and ducked into the night.

Their escape went exactly as he outlined with no mishaps. The guard glanced at his slumped figure and waved them through the gates. The palace had been on high alert today with so many visitors, but most were gone and the security emphasis had been on vehicles arriving, not departing.

After a couple of blocks, Julian straightened in his seat. "You can pull over anytime and I'll drive."

"Oh no. I am having too much fun."

"Katrina."

She sent him a cheeky grin. But refused to pull over. Instead she followed the GPS to the edge of town where she rolled down the windows and punched the gas.

"Whee!" She laughed out loud as she took the expensive vehicle through a tight turn. "I love this auto."

Julian reached across and cupped the back of her head, threading his fingers in her hair. She thrilled to his touch; it was sensual and just a little primitive. Just like the wild ride through the hills. She reached the pinnacle and a view of the bay came into sight. Lights sparkled on the water of the bay, but behind it the North Sea was a vast void of blackness.

"My house is not far. It overlooks a secluded beach on the North Coast."

"We are going to your house?"

"That's the plan." He caressed her neck. "It feels good to be going home."

"I thought you lived at the palace."

"I have rooms there. It's convenient because of the many events I must participate in and when crown business runs long. But I prefer my own place."

"It looks like you will be spending a lot of time at the palace over the coming weeks."

"*Ja*. I will. I'll get used to it."

"Sammy really needs you," she felt compelled to say.

"I have not forgotten. Do not worry, my dove, I will take care of him. We are here." He pointed to a road to the left.

She drove down a long drive to a huge stone fence and an imposing gate. Julian leaned across her to press his thumb against the security pad. He smelled so good she gave in to impulse and took a nip of his jaw, which earned her a retaliatory kiss lethal enough to steal her breath.

"Just follow the lane up to the house," he whispered in her ear before settling back in his seat.

Her hands shook as she put the auto in gear and drove through the gates. After a couple of turns she came to a large two-story white and stone house that blended into the hillside and pulled to a stop in a stone portico. The door opened and a younger version of Grimes stepped out and opened her door.

"Welcome Fräulein Vicente."

"Allow me, Kristof." Julian came around the auto and took her hand. He helped her from the low-slung vehicle. "This is Kristof, my man of all things. He keeps my life in order."

"You give me too much credit, Your Highness."

He ushered her inside giving his manservant a raised brow look that made her think they shared a more informal relationship. "Kris, please bring us a tray of food and some wine. Then I wish not to be disturbed."

"Of course, my lord," Kris responded as he closed the door.

"Oh but—" Katrina dragged her feet. It seemed so rude to rush right off. Heat rose to her cheeks. Especially to the bedroom.

"Come, my dove." Julian drew her forward. "I will give you a tour. You can help me pick out Sammy's room."

"You plan to bring Sammy here?" With the lure

of a tour, she fell into step next to him through the white marble entry. She had assumed he'd leave Sammy in the palace nursery.

"I expect my schedule to be pretty full, but when I can get away, I'll want him with me. This is the living area." He waved her into a pillared room off the entry. A wall of windows brought the sea inside. She walked over to look out and admired the view of the bay. The furnishings were sleek and modern, light on white, esthetically beautiful but hardly child friendly. A fireplace gave the promise of warmth.

"I am happy to hear it. You will both benefit from the contact."

"Tessa asked for her position back," he told her.

A sense of dread welled up. Her stomach knotted as her fears resurfaced. Had he brought her here to tell her she was no longer needed as Sammy's nanny? To let her down easy?

"Your father mentioned she showed interest in returning. He seemed to think Sammy would do well with someone familiar."

"I agree, but it will not be Tessa." He continued the tour as they talked, showing her the dining room, an office, and the gourmet kitchen where Kristof prepared their meal before leading her up an open staircase.

His response had her emotions ricocheting

from one extreme to another in a matter of seconds. "Why not?"

"It was clear her interest was not in caring for Sammy." He gestured to a glass wall overlooking a pool. "The lower floor has a lanai. There's also a gym with a sauna, and Kristof's rooms are there along with additional servants' quarters when they are required."

She bit back a smile. "You mean your security detail."

She should have known he'd see through the other woman's shallow facade.

"They have been used for that purpose, *ja*." He showed her two bedrooms with en suite baths. Both rooms carried on the color scheme from downstairs and were starkly beautiful, but in her opinion the minimalism went too far. His suite was only slightly better in the fact it incorporated some color, gray and blue, and a few personal touches including a vivid painting of a storm at sea. The lavish bath with the large circular walk-in shower was the very definition of luxury.

It was good to be the Prince.

The view from his terrace took her breath away. The bay sparkled to the right, and in the far distance lightning flashed, highlighting clouds and sea as a storm rolled through. At the end of a long incline, waves crashed against a private beach.

"Lovely," she breathed. "You are closer to the coast than I realized."

Hard arms wrapped around her waist and drew her against his aroused body. "On a clear day you can see the British Isles from the roof deck. I'm on an inlet. Much smaller than the bay, but it protects me from the worst of the storms and has the benefit of the beach."

"You have a beautiful home." She leaned back, savoring his warmth. And the knowledge he wanted her.

"Hmm." He kissed her neck. "That sounds like there is a *but* attached."

"I just have a hard time seeing Sammy here. All the white, it is a little cold."

He stiffened and his arms dropped away. He moved to a table next to a two-person lounge and picked up a glass of wine from a tray of food-stuffs Kristof must have left while they were touring the house.

She hugged her arms to herself. What had she said to drive him away?

"Many people consider me to be cold." He sipped the wine, choosing to look at the view rather than her. "*Unemotional* is another word they use."

"Not me," she denied, walking toward him, stopping between him and the view. "You have never been unemotional with me."

"No," he agreed as he caressed her cheek. "You are a meddlesome creature. It is impossible to be unaffected by you."

She wrinkled her nose. "*Mon Dieu,* that does not sound like a compliment. Perhaps you are cold after all."

"You dare much. It is hard to believe you are cowed by a phantom photograph."

It was her turn to move away. "Sometimes our fears are irrational. It does not make them any less real." She stared out to sea, wished the past away. "I do not wish to discuss it."

"I dislike seeing you suffer needlessly. The type of photograph you described is worth a lot of money to the tabloids. If someone had them, they would already have sold them."

"Maybe they do not know who I am, or maybe they are waiting for me to gain in notoriety to drive the price up." Seeking to distract him, she turned and looped her arms around his neck. "We could play the maybe game all night. But I did not come here to talk."

Lifting onto her toes, she pressed her lips to his, tracing the line of his mouth with her tongue until he opened and all but consumed her with his immediate response. He tilted her head and deepened the kiss.

And all thoughts of phantom photos were lost under his sensual assault.

He swept her up, making her head spin, or was that just the intoxicating result of his touch. The Fates knew he drove all rational thought from her head. But tonight she didn't care. Tonight was all about giving in to passion, to the needs of her lover.

Lover.

Her mind stuttered over the word. Especially when she looked into the heated eyes of the Prince. Prince. Boy, when she deviated from the norm, she went totally off planet.

She'd denied herself for so long, unwilling to risk a closeness that would shatter the little confidence she'd reclaimed. But Julian's grief ignited her compassion, allowing him to breach the wall she'd built around her emotions and reach her vulnerable heart.

He set her on the lounge and joined her. Built for two, his bulk made it a tight fit, but she didn't mind. Her body took over, putting a brake on the rising panic. She didn't mind at all. The closer the better.

Yes, she shivered as he traced his hand over the curve of her hip. She'd worry about emotion tomorrow. Tonight was about sensation, about forgetting, about touching the stars.

"Are you cold?" He broke off the kiss to reach for a blanket, pulling it over the both of them.

"Not in the least," she assured him. But she

spied the tray of food behind him and on cue her stomach rumbled. "Goodness." She lifted one shoulder in a sheepish half shrug. "But I am hungry. I only picked at the food at the reception. Can we see what Kristof left for us?"

"But of course." He lifted the heavy tray with one hand and placed it on their laps. It contained roast beef, a choice of cheeses, soft bread cut into slices, some fruit and an assortment of biscuits.

"Oh my. This is a feast." She fed him a grape.

He chewed then selected a roll of thinly sliced roast beef, but after a few minutes she realized she was the only one attacking the tray of food.

"You are not eating."

"You made me eat at the reception. Plus, I am enjoying watching you." He ran the back of his finger along the line of her jaw. "There is only one thing I am hungry for."

Heat bloomed under the intensity of his gaze. His thoughtfulness in the face of his desire touched her. First he protected her from the cold and then he fed her, all while putting his passion on hold.

How could she have thought him cold or unfeeling?

Yes, there was a necessary reserve he kept between himself and the world, but a royal learned early in life that a certain level of distance was needed to retain any sense of self. Add Julian's natural inclination for order and control, his penchant for numbers and strategy, and his impatience with fools and incompetence, and it stood to reason he projected a cooler demeanor. It didn't make him cold.

His explosive passion taught her that.

More, the man cared, for his nephew, for his family, for his country. Perhaps too much. For all his cool reserve, he gave his full attention to whatever was before him. Nobody could fault him on his dedication.

And right now, all that lovely attention was focused on her.

She took the tray and leaned across him to set it on the table, then she stood and held out her hand. "Come. Let us feast."

Taking her hand, he surged to his feet and pulled her to him, claiming her mouth in a kiss that demonstrated just how hot-blooded he was. He took and she gave, her surrender becoming its own demand, for more, for hotter, for him.

A breeze blew a fine mist over the terrace. She gasped, the cold water a shock against her over-heated skin.

"The storm is getting closer." She snuggled into Julian's warmth.

"Sometimes I like to sit out here and watch the storm roil across the sky. But not tonight." He solved the problem by sweeping her into his arms and stepping into the room. "Tonight I want to watch your face as the storm we create flashes through your eyes."

"Feast and storms," she teased, looping her arms around his shoulders. "Sounds like a soggy picnic."

He threw back his head and laughed. "So much for romance."

"I do not need romance." She stroked his jaw. "I prefer honesty."

"I, too, detest games."

"I know." She sighed as he set her on her feet beside the bed. "You are the most truthful and honorable man I know. Our time together is so limited." Her fingers went to the buckle of his belt. "Let us not waste time. Make love to me."

He caught her fingers, brought them to his mouth for a brief kiss. "You make me want to linger, to play. No time with you is wasted. I speak the truth when I say I want to watch you ignite in my arms."

He placed her fingers on the top button of his shirt then his went to work on hers. "I agree the time for talk is over, but I will not be rushed." He bent his head to nibble the exposed curve of her neck. "I intend to take my time."

So that was his plan. To take his time. He'd certainly been doing that. Giving her the tour, feeding her, all the while seducing her with soft touches and heated kisses. Slowly, surely, he'd gotten her all worked up. And now he wanted to put the brakes on again? No.

"Then we are at odds, lover." She grasped the edges of his shirt and pulled with all her strength. Buttons flew in every direction as the hard planes of his chest were revealed. "Hmm." She hummed her approval. "You take your time, but I am done waiting." And she dived in for a taste of all that yummy skin.

The muscles under her lips moved as he chuckled. "So contrary. You go at your pace and I'll go at mine." He lifted her head to press a kiss to her lips. "I am sure we will meet up in the middle."

She smiled and nipped his bottom lip. "Get naked. Now."

Surprisingly—considering his slower agenda— he complied. He shrugged out of his ruined shirt, stepped out of his pants and briefs. His socks flew over his shoulder and then she was finally in his bed. And while he slowly undressed her, she trailed her hands over every muscle and bulge, enjoying the feel of him, smooth in some places, hair roughened in others.

Every caress led to a need for more. Everything about him was vital, resilient, addicting. He was all male and he made her feel alive, feminine, empowered.

But with every slow, deliberate touch, she felt a

growing urgency. Even as she clung to him, time seemed so short. If this night was all they had, she couldn't waste a second.

She arched under the soft caress of his hands. With deliberate, unhurried determination he stripped her, carefully leaving her nearly sheer cotton camisole, and then proceeded to trace the curve of her body until he cupped her breasts under the soft fabric. With loving, torturous precision, his mouth tormented the tips through the cloth bringing her exquisite pleasure.

Okay, that slowed her down. Kind of hard to seduce him while she soared on sensation. Then again, maybe this was where they met up. He certainly had her attention. She dug her nails into his back and lifted into his touch, pushing her breast into his hand, wanting more, wanting it harder.

He didn't disappoint. But neither did he hurry.

"Beast," she taunted him. "Stop teasing me."

"Not teasing," he breathed against her ear. "Pleasing."

"Not fast enough."

"Why are you in such a hurry?" He slid his hand down her hip. "We have all the time in the world."

"But we do not," she corrected him. "Time is slipping away. We must hurry or we will lose this opportunity."

"Not a chance."

"But—"

"Shh, my dove. We have all night. And I won't be rushed."

How could he be so calm? "You could get called away at any minute."

"Is that what you're worried about? No need." He trailed his mouth along her collarbone. "No one will disturb me short of World War Three."

She pulled back, her eyes going wide. "*Mon dieu*, we have just jinxed the world."

He laughed, causing his body to rub against hers in interesting ways. "You are such a delight." A hard kiss destroyed her thought processes. "If this is the end of the world, then let us make it worthwhile."

"If this is the end of the world—" she rose up, and biting her lip, pulled her camisole up and off "—then I do not want anything between us."

His eyes glinted in approval, easing her anxiety. He rose up next to her, drawing her to him, offering her the shelter of his arms, replacing fear with wonder.

Sighing, she gave herself into his care.

His talented fingers sent her body arching again. His reverent touch making her feel cherished. And still he would not be rushed. Darn him. Her nerves sizzled. What he did to her defied rational thought. He went to her head like the finest champagne, making her tipsy on sensation.

Still a novice at lovemaking, she mimicked his every caress, doing unto him what he did to her, and soon she experienced the thrill of having him on the brink of losing control. He joined them with more urgency than care, and she loved how driven he was.

She wrapped him in her arms and rode the storm, feasting on his cry of fulfillment. And when the world exploded in a prolonged moment of bliss, World War Three could be raging outside and she wouldn't even know.

CHAPTER ELEVEN

DAWN JUST TOUCHED the horizon when Katrina strolled with Sammy onto the terrace for breakfast a week later. Disappointment bit deep when she saw the empty chair at the head of the table. No Julian.

She hoped he was only running late. This time alone with him—well, except for Sammy—had become a favorite time of day. Superseded only by the passionate nights when he managed to steal through the secret passage to light up her world.

The time was fast approaching for her to leave. Sammy had taken to Inga. And though he still ran to Katrina, the time would soon come when delaying her exit would be more detrimental than beneficial.

A maid arrived with a tray of food. She set it in the middle of the table, nodded and retreated.

Katrina had made two official appearances with Sammy, one with Giselle at a hospital luncheon and one with the royal family as King

Lowell accepted a Cross of Saint James awarded to Donal for his dedicated service to the Kardanian Armed Services. It was the highest honor a soldier could receive.

There hadn't been a dry eye at the ceremony, except for Sammy, who didn't understand. He'd been more upset by her tears than by the accolades heaped on his father. With the resilience of the very young, he was already moving on. Yes, he still missed his parents, but he was more concerned with what was in front of him than in those beyond his reach. It was both sad and encouraging.

And ultimately the best thing for Sammy.

She'd helped him through the transition, but soon she would become a part of what he needed to set aside in order to move forward.

But she wasn't ready to go.

She glanced at the terrace door, hoping to see Julian appear. This past week had been the happiest of her life. Not even having the press latch onto her connection to Jean Claude could dim the joy she took in Julian's arms. And the attention hadn't been that bad. The connection seemed to legitimize her presence at the funeral, and she was praised for her assistance during a difficult time.

Julian was quick to point out she'd worried over nothing.

She sighed. So far.

When everything was so good, she couldn't help worrying something would come along to spoil it.

"Where Unca Julie?" Sammy demanded. He did enjoy his mornings with his uncle.

"Uncle Julian is a busy man." She dished some hot cereal up for the boy and set it in front of him. "Hopefully he will be here soon."

Sammy nodded and dug into his food. Katrina waited for Julian for a few minutes but when he didn't appear, she made herself a plate of eggs and rashers and a bit of toast. After she caught herself glancing at the door for the third time, she reached for the paper set on the table in front of Julian's seat.

She flipped it open and froze. The paper shook until she dropped it onto her plate of half-eaten eggs. It wouldn't matter. She felt sick. She buried shaking hands in her lap as she reread the headline.

PRINCE JULIAN GRIEVES IN THE ARMS OF JEAN CLAUDE'S GOD-DAUGHTER. IS THERE A ROYAL WEDDING ON THE CARDS?

Under the caption was a picture of Katrina locked in Julian's arms. They were kissing, his hair was tousled and her clothes were in disarray. It was more than clear what they'd been doing and what they intended to do. They were on the balcony of Julian's home.

The blood drained from her face leaving her light-headed. She closed her eyes, unable to look at the picture of a special moment turned ugly. This was what she'd feared, becoming a public embarrassment.

It tore her up, knowing her father would see the image. And Jean Claude. And Bernadette. Worse, Julian and King Lowell had probably seen it. Was that why Julian wasn't at the table?

Of course it was. He was probably working on damage control right now.

No need to read the article.

Her stomach churned and spots formed before her eyes. Frightened because Sammy was there, and she was responsible for his care, she scooted back and put her head in her lap. Immediately the dots began to fade.

"K'tina okay?" Sammy climbed off his chair to pet her hair.

Great, a young child was comforting her. That really spoke to her state of mind.

Pulling herself together, she lifted her head and gave him a weak smile. "I am fine. Just a little tummy ache."

"You need medcin?" he asked, worry puckering his little forehead.

Damage control. That's what she needed, action to replace the helplessness that nearly incapacitated her from the moment she saw the newest life-destroying photo.

"No. Medicine will not help me." Her heart wrenched at his obvious concern. He was such a sweet boy, and the whole world now believed she'd used him to get to his uncle. The situation was intolerable. "Come on. Time to return to the nursery."

After dropping Sammy off with Inga, Katrina returned to her room and went straight to the secret passageway. This was the first time she'd used it without Julian, but she found the hidden lever and the door swung silently open.

A little nervous, she stepped inside. She remembered Julian pointing out his office when they were making their escape the night of the funeral. She hoped she could find her way.

The last thing she wanted to do was publicly approach his office. Not now the whole of Kardana knew they were lovers. The need for discretion became imperative as the forbidden embrace posted in full color flashed before her mind's eye.

Quickly making her way along the narrow corridor, she found the stairs and went down two flights then took the first passageway on the left.

She hadn't noticed the two times she was with Julian—the night of their escape and the memorable night he'd insisted on having her in his bed—just how many passages made up the inner workings of the castle. A person could seriously get lost in here.

Actually the prospect didn't overly worry her at the moment. In fact, disappearing held a certain appeal.

Except she wasn't that big a coward.

Keeping a low profile to prevent episodes such as this was one thing, leaving others to clean up her mess was another. She'd allowed her father and Jean Claude to call the shots three years ago because she'd been a traumatized innocent, but now she was an adult. She was responsible for her own actions.

She warned Julian this could happen, yet she'd let him seduce her into believing they were safe tucked away at his home. This just proved there was nowhere the press couldn't reach with their high-tech cameras.

At the third door down, she paused to listen. Nothing. Did that mean he wasn't in there, she had the wrong room or perhaps the rooms were soundproofed? Given the delicate nature and highly confidential conversations that took place in these offices, she suspected the third option.

Mon Dieu, that meant she'd have to open the

door to discover if Julian was inside. Crossing her fingers, she turned the knob and inched the door forward.

"Marriage?" Julian's voice.

She sighed, thank goodness. She pushed the door another inch and froze. From the small view of books and statuary she knew immediately she had the wrong room.

"Really, Father, when did you start believing the headlines?" The derision in Julian's tone stung. She more than anyone knew the headlines were a gross overstatement of the situation, still she had hoped for a little sympathy.

She backed up, intending to leave, but the sleeve of her sweater caught on the doorjamb. She tugged, but it held. Unfortunately, it was her right arm and she couldn't see where it caught.

The conversation in the room continued.

"I am not talking about the headlines. Though you should know the reaction of the people is quite favorable. They are pleased at the notion of a royal romance."

"Romance always catches the imagination of the people," Julian said dismissively. "It will pass as all gossip does."

Was it really that easy for him? Had he not considered her position at all? Katrina struggled with the captive threads. The sweater was already snagged beyond repair, but she dare not pull free and leave evidence of her presence behind.

"You deliberately misunderstand me. I am talking about a serious romance resulting in a real marriage creating a family for you and Samson."

"You're suggesting I get married to provide Sammy with a new mother?"

"My son, we have seen how fragile life can be. I am telling you it is your duty to marry and provide an heir."

"You have two...that's usually considered enough."

"Do not get flippant with me. This is important."

"This is too much." The movement of Julian's voice indicated he'd risen to pace. "I have all I can handle. I have neither the time nor the inclination to look for a wife."

Mon Dieu, that stung, too. For no good reason. She'd never presumed to think their relationship would go beyond this time and place.

Liar, her conscious scolded.

And, oh lord, it was true. She lost her heart to him when he asked her to hold his hand on the train. His vulnerability in that moment touched something deep within her. She'd been his ever since.

"You found the time to be with Katrina," King Lowell pointed out.

"You begrudge me a little distraction?" Frustration frayed Julian's control.

"Only when it comes at the expense of an international incident."

"Jean Claude is a friend. He knows I would never hurt Katrina."

Really? Katrina bit her lip. She wished she were so sure.

"Uh!" Her breath caught as she pricked her finger on the stubborn splinter holding her confined. Then suddenly the material gave and she was free. She checked to be sure no threads were left behind before fleeing to the safety of her rooms, tears staining her cheeks.

"Jean Claude is a friend. He knows I would never hurt Katrina," Julian claimed, making a mental note to return his friend's call as soon as he finished with his father. Which he prayed would be soon. This ridiculous conversation was a waste of his time. He would not be pressured by his father or anyone when it came to choosing a wife.

Hell, there were days since the crash when he felt like he had to schedule time to breathe.

The only peace he had these days were the scant hours he spent in Katrina's arms. In those precious minutes he felt no demand for his attention, no political pressure, no claim of duty, no need to be "on." She accepted him for himself and gave freely of herself.

He lacked any desire to hurt her. And even less to replace her.

When he saw the picture in the paper this morning, he knew it was bad. Knew Katrina would freak and his father would disapprove. The one thing he hadn't anticipated was a demand from the King to marry and provide a family for Sammy.

He should have. His father had been showing his fear of mortality lately. Muttering fatalistic comments and pulling back from his duties. Donal's passing only made it worse.

Julian refused to be the next victim.

"I would rather not test the theory of friend over family." Agitation lent a rosy hue to Lowell's pale features as he rejected Jean Claude's goodwill. Pulling rank agreed with him. He looked more robust than he had in months. "If you are not serious about the girl, send her home."

No!

The muscles in Julian's shoulders tightened. In full revolt he informed his father, "Out of respect for you as my father and my King, I have allowed you to dictate many things in my life. Who and when I marry is not going to be one of them."

"Julian, life is rarely fair. I know much is being asked of you, so I will drop it for now." Unperturbed by Julian's bid for independence, Lowell leaned back in his desk chair. "I have no doubt you will do your duty to the crown. The people and the press will serve as my heralds until you do."

"You forget, Father. I am a champion at ignoring the press." His reputation for being cold had been well earned in that regard. Finally it served a purpose. He observed his self-satisfied parent with narrowed eyes. "Since you are in fighting form this morning, you may take the meeting on educational reform. Speaking of duty, it's time you picked up some of the slack around here."

Leaving his father sputtering his outrage, Julian departed the King's office. He was late for breakfast with Katrina and Sammy. He reached the terrace to find their places cleared. Only his setting remained, sans the standard copy of the paper.

As he stood viewing the table, Grimes arrived with a folded copy of the paper on a tray.

"Sorry, my lord. Ms. Vicente quite destroyed the first copy."

Damn. He wanted to be with her when she saw the picture.

"Did she appear upset?" he demanded.

"Yes, she seemed quite distressed when she left here with Master Samson about twenty minutes ago."

"Thank you." Julian turned for the door.

"My lord," Grimes protested, "your breakfast."

He wasn't hungry. But he'd also learned long days required constant refueling. Julian swung back, grabbed a croissant, tore it in half and stuffed it with eggs and sausage. As he passed Grimes, he instructed, "You may clear the table."

On his way to the nursery he tagged Neil on his mobile phone. "Where is Katrina?"

"She's in the gym."

"Thanks." He adjusted his direction. Of course she went to the gym. She worked out daily. And the Lord knew he understood the need to pound out your troubles.

"My lord—" Neil caught Julian before he disconnected "—security picked her up in the passageway next to the King's office about ten minutes ago."

"Sh—" He bit off the profanity. "I'm going to the gym. See that we are not disturbed. Advise Carl my father will be taking the early meeting."

"The press secretary—"

"Everything waits."

"Yes, Your Highness."

Julian ended the call as he entered the gym and turned into the men's locker room. If he was going to go a few rounds with Katrina, he needed to be dressed for success.

* * *

Katrina landed a roundhouse kick in the center of the punching bag. It required little style but provided a satisfying impact. She followed up with a two-one punch. Yah, yah.

Pulling back, she swiped at her cheek with her arm.

Foolish girl. The gym was no place for tears.

She struck at the bag again. And again. Anger at her self-deception burned in her gut. Had she learned nothing from her past experience? Just because she had feelings for a man didn't mean he returned her regard. Obviously far from it.

At least Julian hadn't betrayed her. Small compensation as she dealt with the fact her feelings for the photographer were a mere pittance compared to what she felt for Julian. True love made a mockery of simple infatuation.

The incident in her past paled next to the heart-wrenching pain she currently fought to contain.

The disdain and frustration in Julian's voice as he dismissed any involvement between them echoed through her mind. He obviously didn't love her, yet she'd believed he held some affection for her.

Never had she felt so alone.

She abandoned the punching bag and sought to regain some sense of self by going through the discipline of her regular karate routine. She took a couple of deep breaths before beginning, flowing from one movement to another with rigid control, focusing mind and body on form and motion.

She'd need all her wits about her when the repercussions of the photo in today's paper began to rain down on her. If any pictures did remain from her past, now would be the time for someone to score big. Her name had been linked to two royal houses and she appeared to be the lover of a Prince. A compromising picture of her would be worth hundreds of thousands of dollars. If not more.

She should have stayed hidden in Pasadonia.

Halfway through the routine she became aware of Julian standing on the periphery of the mat. She ignored him in the hopes he'd go away.

He didn't. He let her get through the routine and then he stepped onto the mat.

"Nice moves," he said. "Excellent timing and balance."

She completed two more punches before replying. "I practice often." Without looking at him, she moved right into some quick kicks.

"You're upset."

She had no answer for the obvious.

She wondered at his conciliatory tone. Was he not upset?

"Katrina, I'm sorry you were alone this morning when you saw the paper."

"It does not matter." She gave him the truth. What difference would it make if he'd been there? None. The picture would be no less devastating with him by her side. And given what she'd heard she wondered how sincere his concern would have been?

He appeared in front of her, deftly catching the fist flying toward his face. "I need you to stop and talk to me."

In a flash, her pain turned to anger. He became her adversary. She retrieved her hand, reset her balance and attacked with a few round kicks that made him retreat. "I sent you sprawling to the athletic mat before, Your Highness. Perhaps you should leave."

"Katrina, we have much to speak of."

"Funny, I cannot think of a thing."

"I can be just as stubborn as you. I'm not leaving until we talk." He gracefully advanced on her. For the first time she noticed he wore gym clothes. He bowed formally and took up a basic karate stance. "I know you expect the photos from your past to make an appearance. That's not going to happen."

"So you have said. I can only pray you are right." She responded to his bow and immediately went on the offensive.

His defense and counterattack were perfect. She instantly recognized anger had affected his skills in their last bout and stepped up her game. She wouldn't make the same mistake. He had reach and strength on his side, but she had finesse and agility on hers.

Plus she was stronger than she looked. She made him sweat. Better, she made him breathless, which made it difficult for him to talk. She struck with an open palm, driving her point to the heart.

The next few minutes were spent in physical exertion as she fought to put him on his ass again.

It may be petty, but being dismissed as a distraction did that to her.

The longer they fought, the fiercer she became. Perspiration dewed her skin, stung her eyes, weakened her. Whereas the sweat caused his T-shirt to cling to taut muscles. The harder he fought, the better he looked. Bastard.

Grunts and yells filled the air along with the smack of skin on skin. Fury propelled her actions, but his reckless grin put her over the edge. She finally put him down, but he took her with him. She landed on his chest with a breath-stealing thud and a nasty sense of déjà vu.

Pushing against the granite planes of his chest, she fought to right herself. The hard circle of his arms kept her pinned in place.

"Let me up," she said, careful to keep all emotion from her voice.

"Not until you listen to me." He tightened his hold. "You expect the worst. But don't you understand? When the infamous photos don't appear, you'll finally be free."

"You sound awfully certain." She knew better. Her only chance at certainty was lack of exposure. And that option was now lost to her.

"It just makes sense," he said, his arrogance showing.

"None of this makes sense. Why would a paparazzo wait to sell a picture of us? The photograph in the paper was from the night of the funeral, more than a week ago. And your balcony overlooks the sea. The angle of that shot would have to come from the water." She dug her elbow into his sternum almost earning her freedom. "It is a near-impossible shot."

"Katrina." He rolled, putting her beneath him.

"No." She wedged her arms between them. She needed something, anything, to hold him at bay, to keep the pain contained. "You did this."

CHAPTER TWELVE

"THIS IS ALL your fault," she whispered. "Seducing me, making me feel safe, giving me hope."

She knew in her heart she was being unfair. That he meant to reassure her. Too late. Her confidence lay shattered at her feet. She pushed against his chest. "Let me up."

"Katrina, listen," he implored.

"No. Let me go." She attempted to roll him off her. His elegant hands framed her, holding her fast, preventing her from getting away. She went still. Wiggling would only embarrass them both.

"I can't stand for you to hide away from the world because of a past mistake," he explained, staring into her eyes, pleading for her to understand. "You're better than that."

"My life is none of your business." She looked away, unwilling to acknowledge his motives.

"It is as long as you are here in my palace."

"A problem easily solved." She pushed again, harder this time. "Let me up. I am going home."

He loomed large above her. "You aren't going

anywhere. You need to stop protecting yourself and live."

"Easy for you to say." She turned her head away. "My life is not a game. People I care about can be hurt." She couldn't think beyond the rage, the hurt, not with the heady scent and feel of him distracting her.

"If they truly care, they will be pleased to see you free of the weight hanging on you."

As if he truly cared. "They show their love by letting me make my own decisions."

"You mean they allow you to hide in the palace. Such a beautiful prison. I'm surprised you accept it. Surely it is too good for the severity of your crime."

"You do not know what you are talking about."

"I know you are a shining star but you hide in the background, afraid to draw attention to yourself lest you disturb the shallow life you've built around your fear."

Her chest tightened as the truth struck home. Her breath caught. She couldn't breathe but her mind reeled. She told herself her sacrifices were for her family, to prevent further pain or embarrassment coming to them, but in reality she'd just been punishing herself for failing them. What a disappointment she was.

"Katrina! Damn it, breathe." He lifted off her,

dragged her into a seated position. "I'm sorry. I didn't mean—"

"Stop. Do not pretend now." He may be right about her, but it changed nothing. She threw up an elbow to block him when he tried to draw her close again. "Do not pretend you care when I am nothing to you. Your time would be better spent looking for a wife."

He fell back on the mat beside her, nodded as if in confirmation. "You were in the passage near my father's office. You heard him instruct me to—"

"Look for a wife," she finished for him. She didn't question how he knew she'd been outside his father's office. At least part of the hidden passages must be under security surveillance. "Good luck with the search."

"I'm sorry if you were disturbed by what you heard. But you must know you have been a comfort to me. I was in no mood to discuss our relationship beyond that."

His reasonable explanation for what she'd heard did little to breach her anger and hurt. "I believe the word you used was *distraction.*"

"Both are true." He propped up on an elbow, ran a finger down her cheek. She dodged away from his touch. "I told him, forget it, he didn't get to dictate who I married. I'm thirty-two years old.

I will not be told when and whom I shall marry as if I were a callow youth."

"How crass of him to think of Sammy at this time."

He narrowed brown eyes in ire. "Don't you start. With handling my responsibilities and Donal's, plus preparing for the Europol vote, I have no time to think between one meeting and the next. My visits with Sammy have to be scheduled into my day. And you are my hidden vice. I cannot take anything more being heaped on me."

Hidden vice.

She supposed that described their relationship exactly. And it did not have a good ring to it. Partly her fault, she knew. Her insistence on discretion certainly contributed to the hidden part. But acknowledging it didn't matter. She still felt used. Foolish. Shamed.

She'd let herself be seduced again.

Photographed again.

She couldn't take any more.

"Well, you will have one less vice to worry about. I am returning to Pasadonia."

"No." He pushed to his feet, pulled her up, too. He scrubbed his hands over his face, wiped the sweat on his pants. "I'm saying I couldn't think! While my father was talking I simply reacted, pushing back at him, denying all concept of courtship and marriage. Yet as soon as I left him and turned my thoughts to you, it all clicked into place."

"No." Stomach churning, she backed up.

"Ja." He pursued her hands reaching for her. She childishly put hers behind her back as she continued to retreat. He matched her step for step, catching her by the elbows when she tripped on the edge of the mat.

"Do not," she entreated.

"You are the answer, Katrina. You are gentle and caring, smart, funny and sexy. I can talk to you. Best of all Sammy already loves you."

Her heart broke a little with each word. It was all about the convenience, all for Sammy. "What about you?"

He cocked his head, his brows rising in question. "What about me?"

"Sammy loves me. How do you feel?"

His expression cleared. He hauled her close, kissed her temple, her mouth. "You know I care about you. Haven't I demonstrated how much each night in your bed?"

"You want me." She wormed her arms between them, seeking distance, needing the ability to think. "That is passion. It will fade."

"It hasn't," he stated with emphasis. "My need for you has only grown." A finger on her chin lifted her face to him. She stubbornly refused to look at him. "Katrina, will you marry me?"

Her gaze flew to his, and she saw amusement lurking in his amber eyes. Oh God. How sad was it that for a moment joy flared through her? Pretty pathetic, as proven by his humor at her expense.

Oh, she had no doubt he was serious. Lowell's point, after all, had been to provide Sammy with a mother figure. Who better than she? Hadn't she put her life on hold for the child? She loved the little guy, wanted the best for him. But this was one sacrifice beyond her.

"No." Pretending her heart wasn't breaking, she pulled away from Julian. "I am done being used by you."

"Harsh." He reached for her hand. She tucked it behind her. "You love Sammy. We're good to-gether. We can make this work."

"We really cannot."

"Katrina. I want you for my wife."

"No, you want the comfort you find with me. Well, I am done being a diversion for you. You do not get to manipulate my life, turn around and insult me, and then expect me to fall all over myself when you propose. You think you know me and maybe you do, but you do not love me."

Sliding to the side, she gained her freedom, stepped away from him with hands fisted. "In a world where everything around you seems out of control you have found the one thing you can apply reason and strategy to solving. Well, my life is not a game and it is not the place for you to flex your leadership muscles."

Walking to the bench at the side of the room she grabbed up her towel. When she turned back, he stood in the middle of the mat, his features expressionless.

"Goodbye Julian."

Who did she think she was? Julian snarled to himself. He was a bloody Prince. Women didn't turn him down. Not now, not ever. His temper no cooler for a cold shower, he stepped out and grabbed a monogrammed towel.

She should be honored and thrilled by his proposal. Instead she acted as if he'd betrayed her.

Forgive him if he didn't see the tragedy in the photo making the papers. His father and Katrina were both overreacting.

Never a violent man, he'd experienced a rage unlike anything he'd ever known when she told him of how she'd been drugged and humiliated. He'd wanted to hurt someone. Do something. He'd been helpless to defend her.

So seeing her freed from her self-imposed isolation pleased him enormously.

Fury flared as he remembered the hurt and dejection on her face. With a sweep of his arm he cleared his bathroom counter. Bottles, soap, crystal dishes went flying across the room.

He left the disarray and marched to his closet, chose a new suit, a matching tie.

Damn her for treating his proposal as an insult.

So he hadn't been as smooth as he could have been. And maybe he should have chosen a better time. And place. She didn't have to attack his motives, his character. They were good together, both in bed and out. She loved Sammy. Was it so wrong to think they would make a happy family?

It all went to show he'd been impulsive in proposing. Far from the premeditation she accused him of, he'd reacted to her pain, allowing emotions to sway him, which was totally unlike him. When he looked at the circumstances logically, he reverted to the arguments he'd given his father.

He had a country to run. Marriage was a distraction he couldn't afford. The abrupt end to the love affair only proved a relationship was ill-advised at this time. He was too busy for a proper courtship, let alone marriage.

Besides, they just buried Donal and Helene. Bad enough Julian must fill his brother's boots on a political front. It was just wrong to insert Sammy into a new family unit as if his parents were interchangeable.

She wanted to go? Let her. He had more important things to do than chase after an ungrateful brat.

Julian shrugged into his jacket, straightened

his tie and left his suite. Katrina was right about one thing, it was time to put his considerable talents of reason and strategy to work on his country's problems.

Surprisingly, King Lowell seemed sad to see Katrina go. Good manners demanded she bid her host farewell. Giselle gave her a hug and wished her well, but the King showed her to the conversation area of his office and seated her in a Queen Anne Chesterfield armchair.

"I must thank you for all you've done for my family. You made a difficult time more bearable with your kindness and care."

"I hope you might let me visit with Sammy sometime," she asked humbly. "He has truly stolen my heart."

"Of course. Though, I do not think Sammy is the only one to steal his way into your affections. I have never seen my son so smitten." Lowell leaned back in his chair. "Today is the first time he has ever defied me outright." He smiled and shook a finger at her. "He disagrees with me plenty. But he is a strategist. He steps back, assesses. And always he comes with his arguments of logic and reason. Today he argued from a position of emotion."

Katrina fought to make sense of what the monarch said. Had he just confessed to matchmaking?

Was that his response to the picture in the paper? She supposed announcing a wedding was imminent would defuse the sordidness of the situation. Running would no doubt acerbate things, but it could not be helped.

"You play a dangerous game, Your Majesty."

"Julian has suffered much over the past month, and he has much yet to deal with in the months ahead. He would benefit greatly from having a strong woman by his side. One thing I have learned over my many years of ruling—there is a time for caution and a time to be bold, and you must be willing to live with the consequences of the choice you make."

King Lowell sighed, as if some of those many decisions carried some weight. "I wish Julian to be happy, so I felt the reward was worth the risk, but make no mistake there is a duty he must meet here. Sammy will be well cared for, but there is no replacement for a mother figure."

Katrina struggled against a rising confusion. The King's interference may have precipitated Julian's proposal, but the son's sins were all his own.

She knew the importance of a mother's presence in a child's life as she lost her mother at a vulnerable age. Even now she missed her. What she wouldn't give to talk to her mother for just a few minutes. She loved her father, but sometimes she wondered how different her decisions might have been if she'd had her mother longer.

"You are right. Sammy is lucky to have you and Giselle, but he deserves to have two loving parental figures."

For all Julian's faults, he had Sammy on his radar, and she had no doubts he would do right by his nephew. How like him to schedule Sammy into his day. His devotion could not be questioned, which meant he would eventually bow to duty and choose a wife.

She forced the thought of Julian with another woman out of her mind and rose to her feet. Time to go.

"I have taken up too much of your time. I just wanted to say goodbye and thank you for making me welcome."

"You are always welcome here. I fully expect to see you again soon. In the meantime I have ordered the royal jet be made ready and a helicopter is standing by to take you to the airport."

"But, Your Highness!" she protested in shock. "I cannot—"

He held up an imperious hand. "For your comfort, yes. But more for my son's peace of mind. He will not rest easy until he knows you are safely home."

Her last stop was the nursery. Sammy cried. "You go bye-bye like Mama."

"Shh, little man. Do not cry," she bade him. "I will still be your friend. I promise to come visit you." And she would. Soon. While Julian was away.

"No! Do not go," he implored, clinging to her, tears staining his cheeks. His distress wrenched at her already-broken heart.

"I love you, Sammy," she assured him. "You can always count on me. But the time has come for me to go home to my family."

"I don wan' you to go." He burrowed his head against her. Knowing there was no way to make him understand, she gave him a final hug and kiss and then handed him over to the waiting Inga.

"Take good care of him," she urged the other woman. Swallowing down tears, Katrina made her exit, glad to be going home.

The helicopter served as a white-knuckle distraction on the flight to the airport in Newcastle, England where the Royal House of Kardana kept their royal jet. Katrina barely noticed the well-appointed amenities surrounding her in the luxury jet. She sank into a soft cream leather armchair, pulled lush brocade drapes over her window and closed her eyes, shutting out the world.

If only her thoughts were so easy to shut down.

She kept seeing the cold descend on Julian's features as she threw his proposal back at him. She hadn't seen that expression on his face since he accused her of telling Sammy his parents were missing.

He'd been mistaken about her then, and he was mistaken now if he believed she'd be happy in an emotionless marriage.

Loving Sammy wasn't enough. Loving Julian wasn't enough. She deserved to be loved, too.

Longing for home, she prayed Jean Claude's claim was true and that the mortifying pictures taken of her three years ago were well and truly gone. Because more than anything, she wanted her life back.

"Ms. Vicente." A calm voice spoke next to her.

Katrina opened her eyes to see a lovely woman in her forties smiling at her.

"We're about to take off. Please buckle up." She went over a few safety issues, advised the length of the flight then asked if Katrina needed anything.

She shook her head. The only thing she needed was out of her reach.

"I'll check with you in flight," the woman offered and disappeared.

After buckling her seat belt, Katrina adjusted the crystal lamp next to her and reached for a magazine in the cherrywood console, determined to keep her mind occupied with something, anything besides Julian.

She failed, of course. And her spirits were low as she disembarked in Barcelona, the closest international airport to Pasadonia. She'd been informed another helicopter was waiting to take her on the final leg of her journey.

When she reached the bottom of the jet steps and looked up to see where she went next, she spotted the dignified man with dark red hair tinged with silver at the temples. He stood tall and broad, shoulders squared, hands clasped in front of him.

Emotions welled up, lodging in her throat. She flew across the tarmac into the waiting man's arms, felt them close protectively around her. And for that one moment in time everything was okay again.

"Daddy."

"Dear, you're going to have to call him sometime," Princess Bernadette advised Katrina a week later.

"Must I?" Katrina sighed, her gaze following the antics of Bernadette's twin boys as they pranced about the palace courtyard in the early-morning sun. Not even eight in the morning and Julian had called her twice. "He probably wants to know Sammy's favorite cereal. He will sort it out without me."

"Cereal?" Bernadette's stepdaughter, Amanda, joined them on the stone benches. A year and a half ago Jean Claude, and the whole country, had been surprised to learn he had a full-grown daughter. "I'm leaving if you're talking food." The American rubbed her baby bulge. "My doctor lectured me on my weight yesterday so my breakfast consisted of yogurt this morning."

"Pooh." Bernadette waved off the doctor's advice. "Those guidelines are based on an average woman's weight. You are so slim you need the extra calories for the good of the baby."

"You think so?" Amanda asked hopefully. "I don't want to do anything to hurt my baby."

"I agree with Bernadette." Katrina added her support. She'd avoided Amanda because of her notoriety, but Katrina had grown fond of her in the past week. "You are all baby. We can go for a walk after supper if it makes you feel better."

Amanda beamed. "It does. Thanks."

"Yes, well, sorry to disappoint, but there's no cereal. We're talking about the fact Katrina needs to call Julian. He's called her twice already this morning."

"Through his admin," Katrina clarified. "The man can't even be bothered to dial his own phone." That pretty much told her how he felt about her, which didn't amount to much. His real reason for calling was probably to gloat over the fact no pictures from her past had appeared to haunt her. Thank the good Lord.

Of course the press made a whole thing of her leaving Kardana, speculating on the relationship between her and Prince Julian and whether their affair was over or if she'd be returning soon. At the same time they exploited her connection to Jean Claude.

"That is a little punk—" Amanda wrinkled her nose "—even if he is a busy man."

"He would get more done if—"

He stopped fighting his own nature. Katrina barely kept from uttering the words. She bit her lip and shook her head at herself, angry because her first response to Amanda's comment was in defense of Julian.

"—if he delegated more," she finished lamely, which was also true. He might not deserve her loyalty, but she would not reveal private details she'd learned during intimate conversations.

She flushed a little under Amanda's direct regard. "You're not ready to talk to him yet," she declared. "I remember how I felt when I learned Xavier was only spending time with me because he was under orders to keep me close. I felt used and betrayed. I wanted nothing to do with him."

"Yes." Katrina shuddered with a sigh. For the

first time she felt someone understood what she was going through.

"Maman, Amanda," Devin called, "look at me." He did a somersault and landed on his back.

"Me too. Katrina, watch me." Marco outdid his brother by doing two flips.

Katrina and the others smiled and clapped. The boys grinned and frolicked some more.

"It was obvious the two of you were very much in love," Bernadette said. "Just as it is clear Katrina and Julian have something special between them." She squeezed Katrina's hand. "You so deserve to find happiness. Please talk to Julian."

"I will think about it." An easy promise to make as she thought of little else.

"I'm so happy to hear that," Bernadette said. "I feel responsible, you know, for insisting you go to Kardana."

"Do not." Katrina pleaded. "I am not sorry I went—"

"Your Highness." Bernadette's assistant approached. "If I might have a word?"

The Princess stepped away with the woman, viewed something on the tablet she carried. Bernadette's gaze lifted to meet Katrina's. Bringing the tablet with her she handed Katrina the digital device.

"This is why Julian is calling."

The screen was fixed on a tabloid site boasting a picture of Katrina and Jean Claude holding hands in the palace portico. The headline read:

KATRINA RETURNS TO PASADONIA.
IS SHE EXCHANGING ONE PRINCE
FOR ANOTHER?

CHAPTER THIRTEEN

KATRINA STARED AT the shocking headline. She had accompanied the twins as they saw their father off to a meeting, and Jean Claude had grabbed her hand and drawn her outside to ask how she was settling back into the palace.

"Katrina, I'm so sorry," Bernadette said. Behind her, Amanda ushered the boys inside with the help of the assistant.

"No." Katrina shook her head. "I am sorry. I brought this to your family."

"Don't you dare blame yourself for the shameful behavior of the paparazzi." Bernadette's temper flared. "You have suffered so much, but you can't give them power over you. Anyone who knows you will see it for the rubbish it is. For the rest, most people know these tabloids are more fiction than fact. Trying to fight them would only draw out the sensationalism."

"I know, but I hate that you and Jean Claude are drawn into my drama."

"Dear, if not you, it would be someone else.

Jean Claude is the trifecta for the paparazzi. He's a royal Prince, a world leader, a handsome celebrity. He will always be a prime target. As his goddaughter, that attention is extended to you."

Katrina knew Bernadette spoke the truth. Coming out of the shadows meant dealing with the press.

Her mobile phone beeped indicating a text message. Meeting Bernadette's gaze, Katrina reached for the phone. "Julian again."

The text read: ANSWER YOUR BLOODY MOBILE.

On cue the phone rang in her hand. This time she recognized Julian's number. Bernadette squeezed her shoulder and walked away, giving Katrina privacy. Sliding her finger across the screen, she tried for casual. "Hello."

"Katrina." Relief and ire both infused the word. "I saw the tabloid this morning. Are you okay?"

"Thank you for your concern. I am fine." And she would be.

"Bloody press can't leave us alone. Why didn't you take my call?" he demanded.

"You did not call." She took pride in the steadiness of her voice. "Marta did."

"You knew she called for me."

"I have found I am not inclined to wait for you." Oh, that felt good.

Silence sounded from the other end. "I do not care for this stubborn streak in you."

"Just because I refuse to be your puppet does not make me stubborn," Katrina protested.

"Woman, you are the embodiment of stubborn. And meddlesome, persistent, smart, giving, caring and sexy. I've missed you." A huskiness added weight to his statement.

Oh, she'd missed him, as well. So much. But she couldn't let the pain sway her. "How is Sammy?" she asked instead.

"Doing well. He likes Inga. He still asks after you. He wants to know if you're ready to come home."

She closed her eyes against the want. "I am home."

Julian threw down his phone and stood to pace. He was an intelligent man. So why did he still allow her to distract him? Why couldn't he concentrate?

A knock preceded his father's entrance into his office.

"Son—" Lowell took a seat in the more comfortable conversation area, forcing Julian to go to him "—I've heard of the tabloid article. How is Katrina doing?"

"How should I know?" Julian played it cool.

As he had done since she left, preferring to keep the fact he was slowly falling apart to himself.

"Because you phoned her up as soon as you saw it." Lowell rode the chair as if it were his throne. He nodded to Julian to sit. "I assume you spoke with her. Unless you lacked the intelligence to call her directly and had your secretary do it. In that case, she probably rejected your ass."

Julian ground his back teeth. He'd been in meetings, damn it. Which he would have happily have left to talk to her once she was on the line. He should be in a meeting now, but bollocks it all, he needed a few minutes.

He picked up the extension on the table in front of him and instructed Marta to push his day back thirty minutes. He hung up on her protest that his flight to the Peace Symposium left in two hours. Putting thoughts of the symposium and the Europol vote that preceded it aside, he sat back in his chair and drummed his fingers on the leather armrest.

"She said she was fine."

"Did she sound fine?"

Julian considered his father's question. How had she sounded? He had to think about it. He'd been too busy fighting the need to see her, to hold her, to analyze how she sounded. Now he did. A little shaky at first, but she'd grown in confidence.

"She did actually." Which drove him a little crazy. An unreasonable response. Why should he care if she missed him? "I told her Sammy wants her to come back," he revealed.

"Ah." His father nodded as if unsurprised, and then he lifted a bushy eyebrow. "You mean you want her to come back."

"Not at all," he denied. "We've been over this. My duty is to the country."

"Of course. It's for the best. What does she have to come back to?"

Julian rocked forward in his chair, buried his fingers in his hair. "I offered her a kingdom."

"Son—" the proximity of Lowell's voice indicated his father leaned forward to speak quietly to him "—to Katrina a kingdom is more a detriment than an inducement."

"Sammy," he said desperately.

"*Ja,* she loves the boy," his father agreed. "But Sammy wasn't enough to keep her here, and he won't be what brings her back."

"She loves me, too. I saw it in her eyes." Those incredible, violet eyes that revealed every emotion. He'd seen everything in the deep blue depths, from disapproval, to amusement, to anxiety, to passion, and yes love. Which left him with the question, "If she loves me, why did she leave?"

Lowell rose and patted him on the back. "Perhaps it's what she didn't see in *your* eyes."

* * *

"Katrina, you look lovely," Jean Claude said as he stepped into the lounge of their shared hotel suite. Looking smart and dignified in a tuxedo, he crossed the beige carpet of swirling leaves to kiss her cheek. "Thank you for agreeing to attend the gala with Bernadette and me."

"The Peace Benefit Gala is a worthy cause." She swirled the skirts of her lavender ball gown. "And who does not like a party?"

"You." He squeezed her hand, drawing her to the comfortable couch to sit with him. "In the past you have avoided social occasions, or stuck to the shadows. Tonight you've agreed to step into the limelight with us."

"Bernadette explained your press secretary felt a public appearance with the three of us would help discredit the image projected in the tabloids." She perched on the edge of the couch. If she sat back in this dress, she'd need a crane to get out. "I'm happy to help in any way I can. Especially as it is my—"

"Stop." He shook a finger at her. "It is nobody's fault. The paparazzi do not need a reason. If they have nothing to report or sensationalize, they will make it up. As you saw earlier this week. Now that you are a public figure, you will be targeted more often. You cannot fight them...you can only put out the image you want to project and hope the world sees the truth."

A public figure? Her? It seemed surreal, but she supposed the fact she received her own invitation to the Peace Benefit Gala confirmed her celebrity. The international event was well attended by the rich and famous, from actual royalty to Hollywood royalty. She pleated the tulle on her skirt. "What if the world does not see the truth?"

"Then that is their problem." His hand settled over her restless fingers. "You cannot let the press rule your life."

"I know." She lifted her gaze to meet his. "I have finally learned that lesson. It may just take a while to get used to it."

His gray eyes smiled. "We will help you as much as we can. Tonight all you have to do is smile and look like you're having a good time."

"I can handle smiling," she assured him. Looking happy might be harder to pull off. On the table her mobile phone vibrated. Probably Julian again. After talking to him two days ago, he'd persistently called, and she'd persistently refused to answer.

She required distance to get over him. Speaking with him only made it harder to get her emotions under control. Love for him squeezed her heart. If not for him she would never have had the confidence to step out with Jean Claude and

Bernadette tonight. Julian's faith and belief in her gave her the courage to believe in herself, to command her own power.

Tonight she was proud of herself. Despite her heartache, she must put Julian behind her and move forward.

Bernadette swept into the room in a figure-hugging designer gown in a deep ruby red.

"Darling—" Jean Claude rose gracefully and went to her "—you are stunning." He kissed her lightly on the lips. "I will be the envy of every man at the gala." He kissed his wife's hand and wrapped it around his elbow before extending his other hand out to Katrina. "Shall we go?"

Katrina gave her mobile one last glance, lifted her chin and joined Jean Claude and Bernadette on the pathway to her future.

Turned out looking happy came easily enough with Bernadette running an amusing commentary in Katrina's ear as they arrived in the limousine and began the press gauntlet known as the red carpet.

The television entertainment and media magazine professionals were all very positive and friendly, but it was still quite overwhelming. Katrina planted a smile on her face and stuck close to her friends.

Bernadette kept looking over her shoulder. At

first Katrina thought the other woman was just keeping tabs on her, but she finally realized she was watching for someone or something.

"Is everything okay?" she asked the Princess between interviews.

"Of course." Bernadette smiled brightly.

They were a quarter of the way down the red carpet, speaking with a British fashion personality about the designers of their gowns, when Katrina felt the heat of a masculine body slide in behind her and a man took possession of her hand. She knew instantly who it was. The way the fashion announcer lit up only confirmed her guess.

"And we are joined by Prince Julian of Kardana," the pretty blonde gushed. "How cheeky of you to sneak up on us. You look quite dapper this evening."

"Thank you. I'm happy to join my friends for such a worthy cause."

"Yes, it's brilliant to see so many lovely people here supporting peace."

The chitchat went on for a moment more and then Jean Claude led their party off the dais. As soon as they were clear, he offered Julian his hand. "My friend, it is good to see you."

After greeting the Prince and Princess, Julian lifted Katrina's hand to his mouth and kissed the back of her fingers. "I would choose to be no-where else this night."

"Is this part of the plan?" Katrina demanded, pulling her hand from Julian's. She stared daggers at Bernadette. "It would have been nice to have some warning."

"Julian called at the last moment and asked to join us. It seemed a nice touch to bolster the image we were going for. You would only have fretted if I told you."

Katrina was given no opportunity to respond as event personnel urged them along.

She should have expected something like this. Bernadette was happily married. She wanted everyone to have a loving family like she did. And for some reason she believed Katrina and Julian belonged together. Maybe it was that sense of responsibility she'd spoken of earlier for insisting Katrina accompany Sammy and Julian back to Kardana.

She felt surrounded by him. The reporters and cameras all but disappeared as she absorbed his heat, inhaled his scent, melted at his touch. She couldn't look at him, couldn't give him the satisfaction of knowing he got to her.

At the first opportunity she intended to take a firm hand and inform him he couldn't keep disrupting her life with his repeated calls and impromptu appearances. She'd finally conquered her fear; surely she possessed the strength to stand strong in putting their fling behind her.

Julian bent his head to whisper in her ear. "You may take me to task once we are inside."

She sent him an arch look over her shoulder that didn't quite connect with his eyes. "You can be certain I will."

So she smiled some more, talked endlessly about her gown, and carefully remained non-committal to any questions regarding her relationship with Prince Julian. A task made easy as he fielded all inquiries with a brash smile and misdirection.

Finally they reached the entrance and the receiving line. She greeted the dignitaries with somber courtesy and happily accepted a flute of champagne once she entered the ballroom. The bubbles tickled the back of her throat and sent a pleasant fizzle tingling through her.

Julian's hand at her waist constantly reminded her of his presence. A circumstance she needed to deal with immediately. She wasn't an actress. She had no hope of fooling the entire assembly of celebrities and world leaders into believing they were a couple.

"Time to chat." She grabbed his hand and drew him through the throng to French doors leading to a balcony lit by miniature lights threaded artfully amongst the crawling ivy.

He came willingly, practically pushing her out the door. She turned to him, but he was already yanking her into his arms. No time to protest before his mouth slammed down on hers. He ravished her with tender demand, taking the kiss deep. Equal parts possessive and obsessive, he pulled a response from her that had her arching onto her toes seeking to get closer to him.

Or maybe that was just her wanting more of him, reveling in his embrace, sinking into the feeling of safety, and home, and the rush of her blood through her veins as sensation built on sensation and she longed for more.

He nipped her bottom lip. The tiny sting of pain brought her back to her senses. And still it took a moment to gather the strength to push him away.

Finally she created an inch between them. That's all he'd allow, drat the man. And her breasts still brushed his chest with every inhalation as she fought to regulate her breathing, but the space existed, bringing with it the ability to think. Inch by inch she'd gain more.

Her sanity demanded it.

"Why are you here, Julian?" She met his gaze for the first time since his arrival. He looked happy, more at ease than she'd ever seen him. She gritted her teeth. How like a man.

"I'm here for the Peace Symposium. The Europol vote, remember."

"*Oui*. I meant why are your here at the gala? Balls are not your thing."

"You are here," he said simply. "We are on a date. I took your advice today."

"We are not on a date," she informed him emphatically. "What do you mean? We did not talk today."

"Only because you refused to answer my calls." He ran the backs of his fingers down her cheek. "You are so beautiful. A blind date, then. I'm courting you. I meant the advice you gave me about voting with my conscience on the Europol police initiative. I gave my argument and voted accordingly."

"You cannot court me. I rejected your proposal." The urge to hug him had her inching backward. "I am glad you decided to vote from the heart. It was the right thing to do. I can see the peace it has brought you."

"Any peace you see is because I'm with you. Do you realize we never officially dated?" He eliminated the ground she'd gained. "I must court you to change your mind. Turns out others agreed with me, and the initiative was recalled for further refinement."

"And you are celebrating by harassing me?" She took a full step back and came up against the bracket of his arms. Why did he have to make this so hard? Anguish leaked into her next plea. "You need to let me go."

"Never." She was in his arms again, being softly kissed.

What did he mean? Her heart swelled. With fear? With yearning? She couldn't tell the difference anymore.

"Do not play with me, Julian. Not about this. It is too important."

"Why would you think this?" He caught her chin on the edge of his hand, coaxing her into meeting his gaze. "Have I ever lied to you?"

She failed to recall a single instance.

A symphony added background music to their little drama as the dancing began inside. The lilting notes of Strauss's "The Blue Danube" started the event off with a waltz.

He held her close enough to mimic the dance, but neither of them moved as she scanned his face for a clue to his plan. She saw earnestness and sincerity, but dare she believe he cared?

"Come home," he demanded, all playfulness gone. "You belong in Kardana. With me. With Sammy."

"I love Sammy, but he cannot be why I return to Kardana." Bernadette was right, only Katrina could give her power away. She deserved to be wanted for herself, not for her child care capabilities.

"Then return for me," he directed her. "I know this thing with the press is my fault. I should never have brought you to their attention. I thought I was so smart, but I only hurt you. I'm sorry."

"Do not be. If I brought one thing home with me from Kardana, it is a realization that everyone has been right. I have been playing ostrich, hiding my head in the belief if I couldn't be seen, I couldn't be hurt."

"You're stronger than you think."

Wrong. But she refused to live in fear anymore. She was done living in a prison of her own making. Done hiding.

"You believed before I did." Taking back her power allowed her to see he'd been right. "I should have trusted Jean Claude, had more faith in myself." She did not care to be fodder for the press, but she no longer feared her violation would be splashed across the tabloids for all to see. "You have given me a peace of mind I would never have otherwise. For that I thank you."

"I'm glad. The lord knows there's no peace to be found without you. I need you, Katrina. I can't think clearly without you."

"That is only because you are unused to anyone challenging you," she advised him. "You will get over it."

"I don't believe I will," he muttered. "I need you to challenge me, to help me think. To give me the patience to deal with all the people."

"There is only one reason why I would return to Kardana."

"You have only to tell me," he commanded. "I will make it yours."

But he couldn't. There was no forcing love. It had to be freely given or it was not love at all.

"You want my help with Sammy," she reminded him.

"*Ja*. I do. But I was foolish to see that as a reason for marriage. Father put the idea in my head, and when I saw the picture of a future with you, it felt so right I bumbled my proposal by focusing on the wrong thing. And my pride was hurt when you rejected me."

He led her away from the door and the swell of music closer to the balustrade, where he bent down and kissed the curve of her neck. She shivered but refused to be distracted from his explanation.

"Go on," she whispered.

"I love you, Katrina. I may have a genius IQ, but emotions do not rely on intellect. I missed you like bloody hell. I couldn't concentrate. I couldn't sleep. I couldn't get you out of my head. Turns out you were the one helping me keep it all together. You stole my peace when you walked away."

"Julian."

"It took me a while to realize missing you had nothing to do with my pride and much to do with loving you." He brought her hand to his mouth, kissed her palm. The heat of his breath warmed her skin. The warmth reminded her of how caring he was with her and with Sammy, especially when he'd clearly been busy and grieving. And oh how patient and tender he'd been when they'd made love, how he cherished her when she bared herself to him.

"You truly love me?" Hope bubbled through her like the fine champagne she'd sipped earlier. Still, fear made her ask, "You are not just saying so to get me to marry you?"

He grinned at her, a beautiful smile full of affection. "I am saying it because I want you to marry me. But I can wait until I've courted you, until you believe me. I was so overwhelmed with running the kingdom I wasn't paying attention to what was happening with me. I fell in love, but I was afraid to admit my feelings because it was one more thing to deal with. And my brother had just died. The timing was wrong."

"What changed your mind?" Her heart raced as she began to believe.

"Seeing that picture in the tabloids, knowing it would hurt you. It killed me not being able to hold you, to help you through it. You said you were fine, but I knew you were being brave."

"I am fine," she corrected him. "I have decided fear of appearing in the tabloids or the press will no longer dictate how I live my life."

His brown eyes shimmered with tenderness. "I'm happy for you." He adored her with a kiss that went from gentle to heated in a flash. "You will need that attitude as my Princess."

Princess? Oh God. She was in serious trouble, because the notion only half terrified her. She shook her head.

"You are not going to stop pursuing me, are you?"

"No. Loving you, starting a life with you is the most important thing in my life."

"Then *oui.*"

His expression turned half hopeful, half uncertain. "Yes, you will let me court you?"

Happiness was too big to be contained. She smiled and framed his face in her hands. "*Oui*, I will marry you."

He closed his eyes and laid his forehead on hers. His arms tightened to the point he squeezed the breath from her. She squeezed him back. It was impossible to be too close. And then he scooped her up and twirled her around, her skirts flying out behind her.

Suddenly he stopped, set her on her feet and

cupped her face. He wiped tears from her cheeks. "You're crying."

"Happy tears." She looped her arms around his neck. "They are happy tears."

* * * * *

"Now, SEVEN WEEKS LATER, here Abby was with the prince of every woman's dreams riding to the top of the mountain. But there was nothing normal about his life or hers. When she and her father had gone through all the what-ifs before she'd made her decision to be a surrogate, the idea of either Michelina or Vincenzo dying had only been mentioned in passing. But she couldn't have imagined anything so horrible and never thought about it again.

"Shall we go in?" said the deep, velvety male voice next to her.

"Oh—yes!" Abby had been so immersed in thought she hadn't realized they'd arrived. Night had fallen during their journey here. Vincenzo led her off the funicular and walked her through a hallway to another set of doors. They opened onto a terrace with a candlelit table and flowers set for two.

A small gasp of pleasure escaped her lips to realize she was looking out over the same view she could see from her own patio at the palace. But they were much higher up, so she could take in the whole city of Arancia alive with lights for the nightly festival celebration.

"What an incredible vista."

"I agree," he murmured as he helped her to sit. Of course

it was an accident that his hand brushed her shoulder, but she felt his touch like she'd just come into contact with an electric current. This was so wrong, she was terrified.

"Mind if I ask you a personal question?" Vincenzo asked.

How personal? She was on dangerous ground, fearing he could see right through her, to her chaotic innermost thoughts. "What would you like to know?"

"Has there been an important man in your life? And if so, why didn't you marry him?"

Yes. I'm looking at him.

Heat filled her cheeks. "I had my share of boyfriends, but by college I got serious about my studies. Law school doesn't leave time for much of a social life when you're clerking for a judge who expects you to put in one hundred and twenty hours a week."

"Sounds like one of my normal days," he remarked. She knew he wasn't kidding. "You and I never discussed this before, but I'm curious about something. Didn't you ever want to be a mother to your own child first?"

Abby stifled her moan. If he only knew how during her teenage years she'd dreamed about being married to him and having his baby. Since that time, history had been made and she was carrying his baby in real life. *But it wasn't hers, and that dream had come with a price.* How could she be feeling like this when he was forbidden to her?

EXPECTING THE PRINCE'S BABY
by Rebecca Winters is available May 2014 only from Harlequin® Romance—don't miss it!